Matter

OF FACT

The Hart Series
book seven

M.E. CARTER

Matter

OF FACT

The Hart Series
book seven

ONE
Ellery

July

The Maryland file is done and put away. The Julian file is still pending, but up to date. The West's are still sending over paperwork...

Glancing at my desk and around my office one last time, I'm satisfied everything that needs to be done for the day is finished and filed where it needs to be. Having a clean desk doesn't come easy for me. I much prefer to work amongst clutter. However, I've discovered over the five years I've worked as a junior accountant at Welch and Associates, if I come in to a clean desk first thing in the morning, I have an easier time staying focused.

And since I'm up for a senior accountant position soon, I need to ensure I stay focused.

Right now, I'm struggling with keeping my thoughts on track. Not work thoughts. No, those are easy compared to the emotional thoughts I'm having right now.

I flutter around my office making sure the blanket on

the back of my small loveseat is folded and placed just right, and picking up any rogue items that may have ended up on the floor. I know I'm spending nervous energy but I'm so excited for Kevin to come pick me up for dinner.

Kevin and I have been dating since college when we were both on the gymnastics team at Southeast State University. Kevin was always quiet and kind with a sharp sense of humor most people never knew he had. He also never spoke a bad word about anyone. Not in public or in private, nothing like the jerks he would hang out with back then. I'm still not sure why he was friends with them in the first place. They were always trashing anyone who didn't fall into some invisible box of acceptable features. It was obnoxious and over the years I watched it do a lot of damage to some of the more sensitive members of our team.

Just because he hung out with jerks though, didn't make Kevin one. He was always friendly and kind. He was reliable and worked hard. He encouraged me to be those things as well. It was all very attractive to me. Is still really attractive to me. Mostly. Like any relationship, we could probably use a little spicing up in our relationship, but who doesn't after seven years? It's nothing I need to worry about.

He and I have a strong bond. And now he says he has something important we need to discuss. That can only mean one thing—he's about to propose.

I've been waiting seven years for this day. I love Kevin and I love our life together. I love working for his family. I love spending holidays with them where everything is decorated to perfection and it always feels classy. Basically, I just love him. But it's been my dream to take things one step further and officially join the Welch family.

I sigh deeply at the thought.

And then I snap back to reality and grab my compact mirror out of my purse. Checking to make sure the coif at the back of my neck is still in place and putting a small dab of pink lipstick on to brighten the color of my lips a bit, I assure myself that I'm ready.

I'm ready to be proposed to and I'm ready to be Mrs. Kevin Welch, Senior Accountant for Welch and Associates. Everything I've been working and hoping for is about to begin. I just know it.

A quick knock on my door has me looking up just as Kevin peeks his head in. The shy smile I love so much greets me and my heart begins pounding at what's about to happen.

"Hey." He slides in through the half-open door and shuts it behind him as I make my way toward him and greet him with a peck on the cheek. We may be getting engaged tonight but I still need to maintain my professionalism in the office.

"Mmmm… you smell nice," I remark and then smooth over the sleeves of his button-down. The butterflies in my stomach begin fluttering over the fact that he dressed up for this occasion. "And you look nice, too."

"I'm probably going out later."

I furrow my brow in confusion briefly. "I thought we were going to dinner."

"I mean, we could." His face flushes with something— maybe embarrassment that he forgot we had dinner plans. "I guess it depends on how this goes."

I give him an understanding smile. He's nervous and isn't sure I'll say yes. That has to be it. I love that about him. He doesn't usually lack confidence, but this is a big moment for both of us.

Grabbing his hand, I pull him over to the love seat and

encourage him to sit down. "Why don't we do this here. While we're both sitting."

He blows out a breath as he settles on the edge of the cushion and I know he appreciates how easily I'm going with the flow. I don't need a fancy proposal with a string quartet and an audience. Or a chef to write those four precious words in fancy sauce on my dessert plate. Or a photographer hiding in the bushes while we take a stroll through a garden of roses in full bloom.

Yes, I may have thought about these things, but I don't need them. I just need Kevin.

He breathes deeply again, and I grab his hand.

"It's okay, Kevin. Whatever you have to say, I'm listening." I make eye contact and smile, hoping to convey all my love and reassure him he has nothing to be nervous about. With the way his body relaxes, I'm hopeful it worked.

"Okay. Ellery, we've been together for a long time…"

"Seven years."

He pauses, mouth open. "Wow. I knew that but I don't think it registered how long it's actually been."

"Yep." I bump his shoulder with mine and say, "The best seven years of my life."

He nods and clears his throat. "Anyway, these seven years have been great. I enjoy being with you and love that you've found your place here." He gestures around the office and I know he's referring to the family business. The family business I'm about to become part of in name as well as employment.

"I love that we have such a great history together and I'd never want to do anything to jeopardize that."

That was an odd thing to say, but nerves will do that to people so I pretend not to notice and allow him to continue instead, my hand tightening in his.

"I've been doing a lot of thinking about the future and what I want for it."

This is it. The moment I've been dreaming about...

"And I think it's time we go our separate ways."

I open my mouth to respond eagerly when his words finally register.

Wait...

Wait... what?

"You... what did you say? I thought I heard you say you want to break up."

He nods but doesn't pull his hand away from mine. Just keeps holding it, like he's the one who needs the lifeline in this moment and he expects me to be the one to give it to him.

I slowly pull my hand back and rub it across my thighs, not sure if I'm trying to wipe away the clamminess I suddenly have or this moment from my memory.

I take a few seconds to collect my thoughts before asking for clarification.

"I don't understand. Is something wrong?"

"Oh! Oh no. Nothing's wrong," he says like that answers everything.

"Theeeeen... why are you wanting to end our relationship?"

"Well, I've thought about it a lot and I just don't love you like I thought I did."

His words sting in a way I never expected. But his nonchalance is what's really throwing me off. His entire demeanor is one that you might see when someone is trying to decide what kind of sandwich you want to order at the local deli, not break up with your girlfriend of *seven years*.

"And how is that?" I ask slowly, almost afraid of his

answer.

"It was just young love and it's run its course, you know?"

No, actually I don't. For me, it was real love. Mature love. The kind of love that puts someone else first and compromises their life to make the other person happy. Like turning down a job at one of the most prestigious firms in New York City making three times the amount she's making now to stay close to her boyfriend whose love has *run its course*.

I'm surprised to realize I'm not feeling hurt right now. I'm feeling anger. Maybe this is the first stage of grief or something but sitting next to him, realizing he made plans to go out after he popped in to break up with me is making me feel what I can only describe as ragey.

I won't give him the satisfaction of letting those feelings out, though. The last thing I want is to come across as the crazy girl and the one Kevin dropped just in time for her to lose her marbles. Even more important, though, I like my job and don't want to lose it because of a lack of professionalism in the office.

Internally, I groan. My job. I work for Kevin's mother. I hope this doesn't affect my ability to get that senior accountant position I've been working so hard for.

Blinking a few times, I push back the few tears that water my eyes. Now that my anger is more under control I'm not sure if those are tears of frustration, sadness, or hurt. Regardless, I won't let them fall until later.

"This just feels like it's coming out of the blue, Kevin."

"I've actually been thinking about it for a year or so."

"A year?" I'm sure the shock is evident on my face as I run through the last year's worth of memories. I thought we'd found ourselves in a comfortable place and were

building a life together. "Why didn't you say anything before now?"

He shrugs. "You know how I don't like talking bad
about people."

"About people or about me?"

That seems to trip him up. Whatever this is, whatever
has happened, I'm not going to get an "It's not you, it's
me" sentence. Because it is me. It is definitely me. And I'm
not sure how to feel about that.

Except… done. I'm done. And I need to leave immediately before my crazy mix of emotions takes over with no
way for me to stop them.

Kevin startles when I suddenly pop up off the couch
and rush to my desk, opening the drawer with a little too
much force, but I won't let him see me cry. I can't let him
see me cry. Not now. Now before he sees his friends and
he tells them we're over.

"Well. I thank you for coming in to tell me." Pulling
the strap over my shoulder, I slam the drawer closed and it
pops back out, nailing me on the knee. "Ow!" I say with a
grimace when the pain registers.

Kevin jumps up and starts toward me. "Ellery are you
okay?"

I hold up my hand to keep him from getting any closer.
"I'm fine. Nothing I can't handle. I was a gymnast, remember? Bruises are no big deal." The giggle that comes out of
my mouth sounds slightly hysterical to me, so I'm sure I
must look crazed to him.

"Anyway, thanks for coming in. I know you have plans
so just lock up behind you, will you?" I slap the heel of
my hand to my forehead. "Who am I kidding. This is your
family's business. Of course, you know what to do. Okay,
bye now."

I scurry out of the room and down the hall, determined to get out of here as quickly as possible. But where am I going to go? My entire apartment reminds me of Kevin—my *ex*-boyfriend. I can't go there.

As the gravity of the situation finally hits me and as if my body recognizes I no longer have an audience, the tears begin to slide down my cheeks.

I'm not sure where I'm going to end up but one thing is for sure—I need to drive.

TWO

Liam

The rotation being forced on my shoulder hurts like a bitch, but I bite back the explications that are on the tip of my tongue. I won't give him any indication of the pain I'm feeling.

"Hurts when I do that, eh?" Harry, our head trainer asks in his trademark Canadian accent. Apparently, I didn't hide my grunt as much as I thought I did.

"It's not bad." I'm lying. It feels really bad. But I don't have time for a rotator cuff injury. We just started our very short off-season and I was dropped from the first line to second before the playoffs because of this shit. I've got a few short months to get myself back up to par, and I'd rather cut off my nuts than move to the third line.

"I can feel you lying to me." Taking his left hand and adding a little pressure to my shoulder, the spot that is tight as a wire, Harry's right hand grips my bicep. There's a pause, enough that I can anticipate the level of pain that is to come but not enough to speak, before he shifts my arm, rotating it in the opposite direction. The pain pierces through my muscles forcing me to suck in a breath. "That's what I thought."

He gently drops my arm and squirts some lotion into his hand. Harry is the only person I know who has a utility belt on him at all times to carry around lotion, but it comes in handy when he needs to massage out some kinks in my traps.

Gripping my shoulder, he begins kneading, applying the right amount of pressure in the wrong spot. It does nothing to relax me but everything to make me clench my fists together so I don't cry out again.

"I still don't think it's a tweaked muscle."

I grunt. "Thanks for the vote of confidence."

"I'm just saying, you're too young for it to be taking this long to heal. I think it's time for an MRI."

Pushing his hands away, I jump off the table and grab my shirt. "No."

"Come on, Liam. I know you're afraid whatever it says will get you benched, but you're playing like shit. You're babying that arm and not following all the way through on your passes. It's making your snapshot slow as fuck. If I can see it from back here, you know Coach can, too."

"Then fix it," I grumble, getting angrier by the second. "Ice it more often or give me exercises to build it back up. Something."

I'm thirty-one years old and am quickly running out of time to stay in the sport that I've dedicated my life to. I can't let an injury, and a ridiculous one at that, take me out. Seriously, shoulder injury? That's just stupid.

"I'm trying to fix it, Liam, but I can't if you don't let us take a closer look. There's only so much I can do with pressure points and cupping. You need an MRI."

Tossing my shirt over my head, I look him dead in the

eye. "I said no."

"Don't make me get Coach involved. You know I'll do it!" he says louder as I ignore his arguments and storm out the door.

Whether it's his job or not, the fucker better not get Coach involved with this. I'll get an MRI when I'm good and ready. Right now is not the time. I just need some ice, ibuprofen, and a good rub down.

Pain still radiates down my arm and even I know I'm lying to myself which pisses me off even more. I shouldn't be resisting so much. If it's an easy fix, I'm suffering for nothing. But if not…

Pushing the thoughts aside I stomp down the hall and into the locker room, running straight into my teammate, Tucker.

Holding his hands up, he looks at me like I'm about to charge him. Who knows? Maybe I will. "Whoa, man. What gives?"

"I don't know what you're talking about." Grabbing some rogue stick tape off the floor, I throw it into my locker a little too hard. It bounces back at me which pisses me off even more.

"Really? What did that tape ever do to you?"

"It got in my way," I growl but make a concerted effort to rein in my temper a bit. Tucker's a great teammate and great friend. I don't need to be taking out my issues on him. He's not the one who body-checked me into that wall last year and popped my shoulder out of place somehow.

"Uh-huh. That doesn't explain why you look like you could throw down at any moment. Do we need to gear up and hit the ice so you can throw a few punches without messing up my face?"

I scowl and drop to the bench, grabbing my stick to

retape it. It doesn't need to be done, but the familiar wrapping motion does more to relax my body than this conversation.

"I'll take that as a no," he finally says when I don't answer. "I have a better idea anyway."

I have no idea why Tucker is so determined to continue this conversation. I'm not good company right now and nothing he can pitch will change that. Only some whiskey and maybe a woman will help tonight.

"I will allow you to grill me up some grass-fed steak with that spicy homemade marinade…"

I snort a humorless laugh. Tucker is always trying to get me to cook for him. Somehow, he doesn't realize my hobby doesn't include feeding him.

"… and then let's go hang at Frui Vita."

Okay, maybe he's more in tune with me than I thought.

Tucker taps his finger on his chin. "I don't think it's Trivia Night but that's okay. We can drown our sorrows in a bucket of Shiner. Maybe see if we can finally smoke Dwayne at pool."

That gets a small, amused reaction from me. From what I can gather, no one has ever beat Dwayne at pool. He's been going to Frui Vita since it opened and long before the current ownership took over. Now it's a premier spot for the professional athletes in the area to hang out away from the public eye, but Dwayne remains. His ability as a pool shark has become the favorite way to haze rookie players on their first visit.

The more I think about it, the more Tucker may be onto something. I could go for some steak. And a night of shooting the shit with other guys who could give a fuck about what I do for a living sounds about right.

Tossing the empty tape roll aside with a much gentler

throw, I finally use words instead of sounding like a Neanderthal.

"Yeah. I can do that."

Tucker claps his hands together and rubs a few times. "Excellent. I'll send out a group text and see who wants to go. But no one gets steak except me."

I nod once and decide it's time to head for the showers. But first I pop four Advil hoping to take the edge off the throb in my shoulder. Mix a few drinks in and I should be able to sleep with little pain tonight. At least, that's my hope.

• • •

A few hours later, we're at our favorite sports bar, our favorite drinks in hand courtesy of the pretty brunette we've all come to appreciate.

"Thanks, Kiersten," I say when she hands me two more fingers of whiskey. The first one went down quicker than I thought it would, but the warmth in my gut is exactly what I needed. Now I feel like I can relax.

"No problem. I assume you want to run a tab tonight?"

I nod in response. "Just don't let Tucker convince you to add his drinks to my account. I'm not paying for his shit again."

Kiersten lets out a hearty laugh. "Kade is still so embarrassed he fell for Tucker's charm."

"Charm?" I ask with a haughty laugh. "That asshole straight up scammed Kade. Poor kid never saw it coming. Hell, I didn't either until it was time to pay the bill. What an asshole." I shake my head but suppress a smile.

I'm not sure how long Kade has been working here, but what I do know is that he's trying to pay his way through college which I find admirable. I was lucky to have a full ride so I didn't have to leave my comfort zone to make my way through school. And considering Kade is a little on the shy side and doesn't exude self-confidence, I'm sure working at a family-owned sports bar that caters to a mostly alpha male clientele is out of that zone for him.

Which is why I can laugh about him getting swindled by Tucker now. The look on Kade's face when I yelled about the bill is not something I'll ever forget. I thought the kid was literally going to shit his pants. But, of course, as soon as he explained what had happened, I turned my anger where it was supposed to be—on my teammate. Who, just laughed, slapped me on the back, and thanked me for a good time. Dick.

"We got it all squared away now, Liam. Even had an employee memo go out about it."

My eyes widen. I didn't know it was *that* big of a deal for him. "You're kidding."

Kiersten rifled around below the bar for a second before slapping a piece of paper down on the counter. It reads, "Don't believe anything Tucker Hayes says about tabs! He's a liar!"

A laugh rumbles through me. "I assume that's Kade's handwriting."

"You know it," she says with a wink before putting the paper back beneath the counter. "And I already got Tucker's credit card on file so if you need some payback… "

I hold up a hand to stop her. "I'm good. I'm still weighing my options."

"I'll expect a full report when whatever payback is all over. Let me know if you need anything else."

She turns away to address someone at the other end of the bar when I call out, "The hubs at home tonight?"

"Even the owner needs to stay home and play dad

sometimes," she calls back before returning to her work.

Swiveling on my stool to face the rest of the room I consider what a nice family they are. It's no wonder we all feel so comfortable here. They even let Dwayne continue hustling people at the pool table every night. Not many owners would put up with that.

Speaking of, it appears Tucker made good on his promise to challenge the pool shark again.

I push away from the bar and make my way to the pool table. There's nothing I love more than watching Tucker get his ass handed to him. This is turning into a fun evening after all.

THREE
Ellery

Wiping the moisture off my cheeks, I try to focus on the road in front of me. Between the tears that won't stop leaking and the deluge of rain outside, I'm lucky to still be on the road and not in a ditch already.

I could go home, but I can't convince myself to hide out in my apartment. It doesn't feel safe there. It feels like a museum of memories waiting to attack the second I walk in.

Seven years. I gave that man seven years of my life and for what? As it turns out, it was for nothing.

"I don't love you like I thought I did," he'd said, making me wonder if I was having some sort of nightmare.

"It was just young love. It's run its course," he'd said, shattering my heart to a million pieces.

Young love that ran its course? We're in our twenties for heaven's sake, not teenagers. Our entire relationship, the career choices I've made, the apartment I chose, even the way I style my hair, all meticulously chosen with him in mind. Because that's what you do when you're in a relationship, right? You make life decisions based on not just your own needs, but the needs of the person you love. You compromise for the good of both of you, not arrogantly plan for yourself with no regard for the other.

Or maybe it's just me that makes selfless decisions. Maybe none of his choices ever had me in mind.

Realizing visibility is getting worse from the storm and my emotions, I know I can't keep driving, no matter how restless I feel. I may be heartbroken, but I'm not suicidal and even in my emotional haze, I recognize road conditions are really bad. I need to pull over soon.

Following the only lights I see, like a beacon to safety, I pull into a small parking lot. It's full of dark-colored SUVs. Weird. I wonder if it's some sort of meeting hall with like-minded individuals inside working together for the good of the community.

"Ridiculous," I scoff. "No one cares about anyone other than themselves these days," I say out loud to no one but myself since I'm all alone.

Alone, because Kevin doesn't love me like he thought he did.

I bite my lip, hoping to hold back the tears. I don't want to feel vulnerable. I don't want to feel lonely. But try as I might, I don't even know if I would take Kevin back. How is that possible? I loved him for seven years and it's as if his harsh words cut off the supply of feelings I had. Like turning the water off under the faucet, there's nothing left to draw from. Or maybe I'm just numb from crying.

I have to stop thinking like this. I'm generally a happy, even keel person. I don't want one traumatic breakup to change the fabric of who I am. Well, maybe after tonight. Tonight, I'll let myself wallow in self-pity.

Looking again at the building in front of me, I squint,

trying to read the small marquee above the door. Whatever this business is, it's all lit up tonight.

"*Frui Vita*. Is this a restaurant?"

A clap of thunder makes me jump and I realize being in my car probably isn't the safest place to be right now. Maybe this is fate. Maybe hanging out in some random establishment that serves alcohol is exactly what I need to get out of my head and distract me from my heartache. I hope they serve alcohol. Suddenly shots seem like a really great idea, and I don't drink.

Grabbing my purse, I swing the door of my very reliable, but not flashy Kia Sorrento open and run for lights. It's pointless. Even parked in the front row, the rain is so heavy I'm drenched by the time I'm standing under the awning.

"Great," I mutter and try to smooth my hair. Not that it matters. The tight chignon I wear to be professional at work isn't going anywhere. No, it just lost any volume I had on the top. Figures.

Sighing, I pull open the heavy door and step inside.

"Whoa."

This is not at all what I expected to find. The large open space has dim lighting, but it's still bright enough to see. The walls are a pale gray with black accents everywhere, including the front of the large bar. Modern furnishings are scattered around the room, inviting people to sit and stay awhile.

All the large vehicles in the parking lot suddenly make sense when I notice the customers. There are lots of couples here, but most of them are grouped together in cliques, and all of the men are huge. Not that everyone isn't huge compared to me. At just over five feet, I tend to dwarf next to just about everyone. But these men are different. Even sitting down, I can tell almost all of them are well over six feet. No compact vehicles for them.

I'm surprised to see the bartender is a woman about my age, although I'm not sure why I'm surprised. Maybe I've been in the corporate world long enough, I forgot other people still work to live instead of vice versa.

Making my way to the counter, I slide onto a stool, noticing how much more comfortable the seat is than I anticipated.

Wow. This is such a fancy place. I wonder why the outside is so dingy and non-descript. Seems like they could get a lot more business if they gave the outside a fresh coat of paint and made the sign easier to read.

I don't notice the bartender, too busy taking in the environment, until she's standing right in front of me.

"Welcome to *Frui Vita*. What can I get you?" I'm struck by how beautiful she is with her long dark hair and lean body. Even the act of tossing a napkin down in front of me seems somehow graceful when she does it. I'm suddenly feeling very intimidated and unsure of myself.

"Um… I think I'd like… uh…" I stumble over my words as I try to remember what, if any kind of alcohol I've tried and liked before. I appreciate she just stands there patiently while I try to decide. "Whiskey, straight up," I finally blurt out.

This elicits an eyebrow raise from her making me second guess myself.

"That's not the right answer, is it?" I ask quietly.

She smiles kindly at my complete ineptness when it comes to alcohol consumption. "There's not really a right or wrong answer but… well… can I ask you a question?"

I nod vigorously.

"You don't drink very often do you?"

My nod turns into a shake.

"And I'm guessing from looking at you, today's been a really hard day and you're just trying to take the edge off."

I release a deep breath, my shoulders slumping. "Is it that obvious?"

"Only because we've all been there. Driving around in the rain so you don't have to go home. Finally ending up in some random bar ready to drink your night away."

I feel my eyes widen. "Really? I'm not the only one?"

She bobbles her head back and forth. "Plus, you've got the swollen eyes and splotchy skin. I hate getting those things."

My hands are immediately over my face, not that they can wipe away the red splotches I didn't realize were there. "Oh my gosh, I didn't know I looked that bad."

"You don't. I promise. I'm just a woman, too. We can see these things in each other." She leans on the counter, fingers clasped together. "And let me just say, woman to woman, whoever he is, he didn't deserve you."

I feel my eyes well with tears again, not out of sadness, but grateful for her kindness. "Thank you. I haven't quite decided how I feel yet."

"You will. In the meantime," she pushes off the bar and reaches for a glass. "I'm going to make you an amaretto sour, light on the amaretto. I know you want to drink your cares away, but I think taking the edge off is probably more your style."

Oddly, I feel some relief that she's not encouraging me to do anything rash like taking shots or do a keg stand or something. Physically, I could do it, that wouldn't be a problem. But I still have to work tomorrow morning. I don't need to smell like stale booze when I walk by Mrs. Welch in the hallway. As it is, I'm not even positive I still have a job now that Kevin and I aren't together. This is the curse of working for your boyfriend—er, *ex*-boyfriend's mother.

The bartender, whose name I should probably ask at some point since I feel like I should know her, places a small glass of yellowish-orange liquid in front of me. I like that it has a small orange slice attached to the rim. It's a funny thing to appreciate, but right now, it seems like the little things are more important than ever.

Taking a sip through the tiny straw, my mouth is flooded with flavor. "Mmm," I remark and take another sip.

"Hits the spot, right?" she asks with a smile, although I'm not sure if she's pleased with herself for having guessed correctly or if she's genuinely happy she put a smile on my face.

"It really does. Thank you."

"No problem. If you need anything else, just holler."

She leaves me to my thoughts that I try to keep solidly out of the breakup zone and fully engaged in observing the people around me. Not only are all the men huge, but everyone also looks like they have money. I don't mean the decent amount I get paid as an accountant, but lots of money. Like in the millions. Their clothes are all high-end and they seem to walk with that swagger of someone who isn't keeping tabs on how much they're spending tonight.

My gaze zeros in on one man in particular. I'm not completely sure what it is about him that draws me in. Maybe the way he's comfortable not being the center of attention while his buddies are definitely vying for that spot. There's a definite calm surrounding him. He's at least six-four. The dark jeans and blue button-down he's wearing show off his broad shoulders and tapered waist. His hair is cropped close to his head and dark scruff covers his face. A

face that has scars and a large bruise on one cheek.
He is both terrifying and sexy as all get out.
And he's walking right toward me.

FOUR
Liam

I noticed her as soon as she walked through the door. She was drenched, courtesy of the downpour outside, her hair pulled back but obviously not how she had done it this morning. Her business attire clinging to her small body making me wonder what is underneath. But that's not what draws me in and keeps me there. It's her eyes.

Eyes that should never be sad but look like they have been releasing tears for hours.

I observe for a while as Kiersten chats with her. The more I watch, the more I want, no *need* to know what's wrong with her. I don't know why it feels like I'd been punched in the gut or why I'm having such a visceral reaction to someone I've never even seen before, but there it is. My physical pain is of no consequence anymore. Her emotional pain is what I'm focused on.

When Kiersten finally walks away, I begin my approach.

From a distance, she's beautiful. Up close, even more so. Her perfect facial features are the kind that would be stunning with makeup or without, depending on her mood. I can't help wondering what her dark hair would look like down. I can only assume it's long. Is it wavy? Straight? Thick or thin?

If I weren't so focused on how her eyes widen when she sees me coming, I'd slap myself for sounding like a love-sick sap. Love-sick is even pushing it. Lust-sick might be more like it. I'm not even sure. All I know is I'm captivated and need to know more about her.

I'm finally close enough that there's no turning back. Not that I want to. No, sliding onto the stool next to her seems like a much better plan.

"First time at *Frui Vita*?"

It's not my best pick-up line, but I couldn't exactly start by asking her who's ass I have to kick for making her cry.

She smiles shyly. Interesting. And a little concerning. In my experience, shy women don't typically visit strange bars alone.

"How do you know I haven't been here before?"

There's a subtle "back off" tone in her voice which makes me happy. She's still got some feistiness left in her. Even if she's full of shit.

"Because we come here regularly and I know I haven't seen you before now."

She looks at me, a cute little crinkle in her brow. "You hang out at bars in the middle of the workweek regularly?"

My eyebrows raise just a touch. "That's a little judgmental, don't you think?"

Her face pinkens and I know I've unintentionally embarrassed her. So she's skittish. Noted.

"You're right. I'm sorry. For all I know, tonight could be Trivia Night."

I bite back my smirk. "That was actually last night."

She looks at me with a question and I can't help my laugh.

"That guy over there," I point to Tucker whose head is hanging low from yet another defeat at the hands of Dwayne. "He's a friend of mine. Loves Trivia Night, so for a while we would come every week. He used to make us wear these ugly neon green shirts to show we were on the same team. We got to know the owners…" I nod in Kiersten's direction. "…who are great people so we can't seem to stop ourselves from popping in whenever we need to let off some steam."

The woman takes a sip of her drink and licks her top lip of the remaining liquid. It's wild how sexy her shyness is. I'm not even sure she's really shy or if she's just had a hard day and is unsure of things. Me included.

"I didn't know this was a family-owned place. I'm glad this is where the storm brought me."

We both look up as the sound of thunder rolls overhead, as if to accept her appreciation.

We listen to the storm for a few minutes, me not wanting to come across too strong and her, well I can't speak for her, but she doesn't seem to mind sitting in silence. We keep our eyes trained on the big screen nestled amongst shelves of liquor. There's a game on. Baseball. I think it's the Yankees versus the Astros but I'm not paying all that much attention. My eyes may be looking in that direction, but every other sense is focused on the woman next to me.

Every time she shifts in her seat, I sense it. Every time she takes a sip, I know it. Every time she takes a breath, I can practically feel it.

"You two okay over here?"

Kiersten draws my focus back. From the way the woman clears her throat, it seems I'm not the only one who was here but not all here.

"Can I have another one of whatever this was?" the woman asks quietly, setting the tumbler down on the napkin and pushing it forward.

"Amaretto Sour? Sure." Turning to me, I notice an expression on Kiersten's face. She knows I don't hit on women here. This is a safe place for the athletes in the area to not worry about groupies and secret photos and undercover paparazzi. If there's a woman here, she's likely attached to someone I don't want to mess with.

But this woman is different. I know it and Kiersten knows it. And I already know she's going to give me shit later for striking up a conversation with a stranger since it's not my typical M-O.

"You want another Johnny Walker, Liam?"

"Yeah. Thanks Kiersten."

"Kiersten?" the woman says suddenly. She cocks her head for a second and narrows her eyes before she seems to have a lightbulb moment. "I knew you looked familiar. You're Lauren's friend." Suddenly excited, the woman points at herself. "I'm Ellery. I was on the team with Lauren in college."

Lauren? Wasn't she a gymnast? That would mean this woman, Ellery, was an athlete, too. Interesting.

Kiersten smiles wide at the recognition. "I was wondering why I felt like I knew you. You look so different in business attire."

Ellery smiles and it lights up her whole face. Gone is the woman who looked sad. In her place is a vibrant, bubbly personality who seems to have no issue chatting up an old friend.

"So, you own this place?" Ellery asks it with a small amount of awe bleeding through her words. It makes me suddenly wonder what she does for a living.

"My husband Paul does. I sort of married into owning a bar."

Ellery gasps, her hands covering her mouth briefly. "Husband! You got married! And the baby?"

Wow. These two really do go way back for her to know about Carson. Even I'm feeling excited about this reunion and I didn't even go to school with them.

"Oh, that's right. You were there when his birth dad died."

Ellery nods with a sad smile.

Now they've lost me. Obviously, there's a lot I don't know.

They continue to catch each other up on the details and I learn a lot of things about them both I never knew. Like how Carson is now in first grade and obsessed with Legos that Paul frequently steps on barefooted. Like how Ellery is an accountant at a small firm owned by her ex-boyfriend's family. Like how Lauren is living with one of the most recognizable football players in the NFL and will be pissed when she finds out Ellery showed up here tonight and she isn't here too.

It's a regular gabfest that I'm happy to observe, rather than participate in. The more they talk, the more the sadness in Ellery's eyes seems to fade away. She was beautiful before, but she's stunning when she's talking a mile a minute.

"Kiersten!" Tammy hollers from the other side of the bar. "Order up!"

Kiersten shakes her head in amusement at the red-headed waitress. "I'll be back in a few to check on you. And Ellery, don't leave until I get your number. Lauren will kill me if she doesn't have a way to contact you."

Ellery nods in agreement and settles back into her seat, leaving us to get to know each other some more.

"You guys have known each other for a while."

She shrugs and gulps down a few more swallows of her fresh drink. "Not all that well. They used to invite me sometimes when they would go out. But I always brought my boyfriend along so I guess I never got to know them more than just on the surface."

Her brows furrow like she's considering what she just said and isn't happy with it.

"What? What's making you look sad again? The ex-boyfriend?"

After another gulp while she considers her answer, she finally responds. "Yes, the… ex… boyfriend. I mean, he only broke up with me today." That explains the sad eyes. "But I guess I never realized how much I missed out on by being with him. It hit me when I was driving. I gave up my dream job in New York so I could be closer to him. And I chose my apartment because it was the one he pre-ferred. But I guess I never thought about all the little things I missed out on. Like having girlfriends and building those relationships."

She turns her whole body to look at me and I can see the beginnings of a tipsy glaze on her face now that her glass is almost dry again. I should have known by her height that she'd be a lightweight. But if she doesn't drink often, she's going to be three sheets to the wind if she's not careful.

"Do you know if Ann… what was her name? Annika!" She tries to snap her fingers together but misses. "Do you know if Annika is still around?"

"Jaxon's wife?"

Ellery's eyes widen. Her mouth quickly follows. "They got married?"

Looking back down at the bar, Ellery bites her bottom lip. I just watch as she processes whatever thoughts she's having, not wanting to interrupt what seems to be very important thoughts. Or swirling drunk thoughts. I'm not sure but, either way, I don't want to impose on them. Watching her brain work is intriguing.

Sighing deeply, she finishes off her second drink and gestures to Kiersten for another.

"I mean I'm sad, yes." She waves her hand like the actual breakup is of no big consequence. "But maybe I'm more worried that I wasted all these years of my life planning for a life Kevin never had any intention of having with me, and in the process, I missed out on everything I really wanted."

My gut clenches at her words and a wave of empathy hits me. Coming to that kind of realization sucks sometimes. I'm also surprised her thoughts are so coherent.

Kiersten drops another drink in front of Ellery but doesn't stop to chat. I don't know if she's too busy or if she realizes we're having a difficult conversation, but I'm grateful she trusts me with her friend.

Turning to Ellery so we're facing each other head-on, knees touching, I do my best to let her know she's not alone.

"When I was in college, I fell in love with a girl. Dated all the way until graduation."

"And you just broke up and went your separate ways because of a diploma?" She lets out a very unladylike snort and picks up her fresh drink. "Figures."

I let the dig slide, knowing it's the booze talking.

"Sort of. My job was moving me across the country and likely would several times in the first few years. She wanted to be a teacher and while they are needed all over

M.E. CARTER

the country, each state would require different certifica-
tions. By the time she would get one, I may be transferred
to another state again. So, there was no real way to guarantee she could do the job she loved if she followed me
around."

"Why couldn't you follow her around instead?"

"That's not how my job works. There are specific loca-
tions and they decide where you go."

"Are you an Army man?" She wiggles her eyebrows
at me.

I chuckle wondering if her question is the result of her
personality or her amaretto sours. "No. Not an Army man.
But same concept. What it boiled down to is our paths in
life weren't taking us in the same direction. Had we forced
the relationship, one of us would have ended up resenting
the other."

"You think Kevin and I forced the relationship?"

"I don't know the answer to that. What I do know is
your life is taking separate paths now. You can't know if
you should have ditched him long ago." Although from
the sounds of it, I personally think she should have. I'll
never say it out loud, though. "Just like I can never know
if I should have stayed with my college girlfriend. What I
do know, however, is I'm happy with my life. From what
I've seen on social media and the few times we've chat-
ted, she's happy with hers, too. We have great memories
of our time together and are proud of what each other has
accomplished.

While you might have been happy with Kevin, I have a
feeling you're going to find what makes you happy again.
It'll just take some time to find it. And when you do, you'll
still have fond memories of him but realize it was time to
move along."

Her hand comes down on my thigh, startling me as she leans in. "You are really wise, you know that?"

Oh yeah. That's definitely the Amaretto talking.

I chuckle. "You are the first person to tell me that. Usually, people call me a meathead."

She looks stunned, like it's shocking that some random dude in a sports bar isn't touted for his wisdom on the regular. I have to suppress the laugh, even as I glance at Kiersten who gives me a questioning look before mouthing *Uber?* I nod in response and turn my attention back to Ellery.

"It should be required learning to hear the deep thoughts of… what's your name again?"

This time I flat out laugh. "Liam. Liam Tremblay. If you ever need my words of wisdom again, you can find me through Kiersten who knows people who know people."

Ellery being the obvious lightweight she is, sways slightly on her chair. "Wow. She knows a lot of people. I like your name. Liam. Liiiiiiam. It sounds very sexy. But you're very sexy so it fits you."

"Well thank you. I like your name, too."

She pops up straight on her chair. "Did you know someone named a fashion line after me?"

"Really. That's very flattering."

"Well, it wasn't *after* me." Her eyes glaze over as she tries to put it all together. "I think it's the designer's last name or something. But it even went to Paris fashion week. You know where I went?"

"Where?"

"New Jersey. One time for an accounting conference. Cause I'm in accounting."

I can't hold back another hearty laugh. It seems Ellery has a sense of humor when she's tipsy which just adds to her attractiveness.

"New Jersey isn't bad. The shoreline is nice."

She shakes her head sadly. "The closest I got to the ocean was a mural in the Newark airport."

"How're you doing over here, Ellery?" Kiersten asks, sliding up to the bar and resting her chin on her fist.

Ellery immediately flashes her a huge smile. "I'm doing great! I haven't even thought about Kevin once." She pauses, her eyes looking around quickly. "Except right now. But it doesn't count because this is Liam and he is really sexy and loves New Jersey and fashion week."

Kiersten purses her lips slightly and I can see the questions all over her face. I just hold my hands up gesturing that I have no idea how Ellery drew all those conclusions, but I find them cute all the same.

Turning back to our tipsy friend, Kiersten snatches Ellery's phone off the counter and begins typing something in. For whatever reason, I'm not surprised Ellery doesn't have a password on the home screen. She seems a little too trusting. It's refreshing to meet someone whose default isn't cynicism, but something I need to remember when she comes here in the future. If she does. I hope she does.

"You're not going to be able to drive home, sweety so I'm ordering you an Uber," Kiersten says as she types. "What time do you want it to come pick you up?"

"I don't know. Can't Liam drive me home?"

I open my mouth to let Kiersten know I'm fine with that idea, but she stops me before I can say a word.

"No way, babe. As much as I like Liam, we're not going to get you in the habit of getting drunk and letting strange people take you home."

I huff, the sting of her comment a little worse than I expected. I get it and she's not wrong—you can't be too careful, but being lumped in with a bunch of douchebags still smarts a little more than it probably should.

Turning to me, Kiersten confronts exactly what I'm thinking. "It's not you, Liam. But if she's anything like she was back in college, and judging from tonight…" we both look over to see Ellery swaying to some invisible beat only she can hear. "… she's still very much the same…"

"Lightweight?"

"And innocent. Not even a password." Kiersten waves Ellery's phone at me before dropping it back on the counter. "Someone's got to help train her on how to protect herself on her new journey in and out of the bars and clubs she should have been frequenting years ago with Lauren."

The idea of Ellery making this a habit without someone there to take care of her makes my stomach hurt. Suddenly the sting of my pride isn't nearly as important as Kiersten's point.

"No offense directed toward you at all," Kiersten continues. "We're just hypervigilant about female safety around here."

I've actually heard that before, just never seen it at play. I guess that's probably because I'm not a woman.

"But I could use a favor if you're willing."

"Sure. What do you need?"

"I can't leave this bar but she clearly can't make it to the Uber alone. You want to escort her out when it gets here? Make sure she gets in safely and the dude knows you have a screenshot of who he is? You know, a little extra scare tactic from a guy of your size?"

"Ooooorrrr…." Ellery interrupts. It appears she was listening more than I realized. "Liam could take me home and I could have my first one-night stand."

Kiersten shakes her head, an amused expression on her

face. I'm the one who answers, however.

"As tempting as that offer is…"

"Because I'm sexy?" Ellery slurs.

"Super sexy when you're drinking," Kiersten answers with a laugh.

"I know right? I feel so free." Ellery begins pulling pins out of her hair, the dark waves falling down her back. It's thick and wavy, just like I suspected. "I should dye my hair. Doesn't that sound fun? Almost as fun as getting in my pants. Right, Liiiiiiiam? Did you know I was a gymnast? I'm very flexible."

That elicits a hearty laugh from both Kiersten and I. Ellery, on the other hand, leans in on me and I don't push her away, content to enjoy the feel of her under the guise of helping a drunk patron.

"You are very tempting." I flash a wink at Kiersten so she knows I'm humoring drunk Ellery right now. "But you are also toasted which makes it a very bad idea."

"Toast!" Ellery yells, pushing away from me. "I need toast! Do you have cinnamon, Kiersten?"

"I don't. But I bet you can make some when you get home."

Ellery's phone lets off an alert telling us the Uber is right outside. I grab it, take a screenshot of the driver and send it to myself. Not only do I have the information, but now I have Ellery's number. I'll text her in the thirteen minutes the app says it will take until she gets home just to make sure she's okay.

Yeah. That's why. It has nothing to do with me hoping to see her again.

I can keep lying to myself, but it's time for her to go anyway.

"Okay, upsey daisy. Your ride is here."

Ellery pouts. "Are you sure I have to go home? I'm having so much fun!"

Admittedly, so am I.

"If you have much more fun, tomorrow is going to be the exact opposite." I help her off the stool and gather her things. "I've learned over the years it's best to cut it off early so you have no regrets."

"Sooooo many regrets," she says with a shake of her head and I know I've lost her to her thoughts again.

It's an easy walk to the car, where the driver is clearly unhappy about driving a drunk home. But seriously, if you don't want an inebriated passenger, maybe don't do bar pick-ups.

Once Ellery is settled, I lean in and look the driver dead in the eye. "Henry is it?"

As soon as he sees my size, his eyes widen. He nods but doesn't say a word.

"I've got all your info right here on my phone." I show him so he knows better than to try and call my bluff. "I'll be calling this lady in twenty minutes to make sure she got home okay. If she didn't, my next call is the cops. Feel me?"

Henry nods again in understanding and I have no doubt he knows I'll make good on my threat.

Turning back to Ellery, I brush her hair back and give her a small kiss on the forehead. "Take care, sweets. I'll see you again, I'm sure."

I wait until the car is out of sight before heading back into the bar, where I wait for twenty minutes to send the promised text making sure Ellery is okay.

Just a few minutes after I hit send, I get her response.

Ellery: I am a-ok, sexy Liiiiiiiiam. ;)

Chuckling to myself, I click off the screen and return to my friend. Turns out all I needed to fix my bad mood was to hang out with a funny brunette accountant who had one too many Amaretto Sours.

I can't wait to do it again.

FIVE
Ellery

I cannot believe I tried to seduce a stranger into having a one-night stand.

Kevin's breakup declaration was barely out of his mouth and I was off propositioning someone else. That's not me! I should be grieving over the loss of the love of my life. Pining over a relationship gone wrong. Eating ice cream in front of Lifetime Movies and Mysteries while I wonder where my life went off the rails.

But no. I was galivanting around town, hitting on strangers.

Yes, it was two days ago, but I can't stop thinking about it and berating myself for my own indiscretions. I'm not the kind of person who can just sleep with someone willy-nilly like that and be okay with myself in the morning. I'm an accountant for goodness sake. I like order and spreadsheets and wear suits and eat brunch with my parents and watch laugh-track comedies and… and…

And holy cow, was that man sexy.

Liam. That was his name and it fit him. After years

spent with the men's gymnastics team who aren't known for their height, his was a shock to me. He was huge. His broad shoulders screamed strength and power. His thighs were like tree trunks in his snug jeans. But his smile. It was electric. It was that look combined with his humor that lowered my defenses.

Well, that and three Amaretto Sours back-to-back on an empty and emotional stomach.

As much as I wanted to stay and drink more, I'm glad Liam put me in that Uber and sent me home. Not only can I not guarantee I wouldn't have made an even bigger fool of myself, but it's also the only reason I made it through the next workday. Even if I've been distracted all day by thoughts of the sexy man I propositioned.

My phone buzzes, startling me from the memories. Good. I don't need to be thinking about these things anyway. I'm at work and I am a professional. I should be focusing on the Smithers account and my final review of their quarterly taxes before filing.

Instead, I slide my screen open and notice a text from an unknown number. The Smithers account is immediately forgotten.

Could it be him again?

No. It couldn't be. He texted me once to make sure I got home okay and I'm sure my inappropriate response will keep him from ever using my number again. I feel a flush of warmth rush through me remembering the embarrassment as I read that exchange with sober eyes. I'm sure he thought I was some blithering, immature idiot.

It doesn't matter anyway. I should be thinking about Kevin. Why am I not thinking about Kevin? The man I spent seven years with. The one who shattered my heart into a million pieces mere days ago. If I'm going to be ignoring my job and thinking about any man, that's who I should be thinking about. Right? What does that say about me if I can push him aside so easily?

Still, what if the message is from Liam?

If I don't read it, it's just going to drive me crazy and then I'll never get any work done. Quickly I open it before I change my mind.

> **Hey, Ellery. It's Lauren from college! Kiersten said she ran into you and gave me your number. Glad to know you're around! Was hoping you'd like to meet us at the bar again tonight to catch up. Annika will be there. Remember her? Amaretto Sours are on me! Lol**

I can't believe Kiersten told her about the drinks. I'd be slightly embarrassed except it's Lauren texting me. Back in college, she had no inhibitions whatsoever. Even when the rest of the team hated her for it, she didn't care.

I always admired that about her. Maybe that's why I always forced her to be my friend on the team. Not besties but someone to hang around during our downtime. I was hoping that confidence would rub off on me. It didn't, but at least I had someone to talk to.

Lifting my thumbs to reply, I glance up when someone knocks on the door of my office.

Unexpectedly, Kevin pops his head in. "Hey Ellery. Just wanted to see…" He pauses, taking in my appearance. "What happened to your hair?"

Any butterflies in my stomach that may have been taking flight at his unexpected presence immediately die a quick death.

I clear my throat and sit up straight, placing my phone face down on my desk.

"I'm told this version of lavender gray is very trendy right now."

For whatever reason, I decided to dye my hair last night. Probably because this is my first ever breakup and I just couldn't not do it. I mixed something wrong though, although I'm still not sure what, and I was mortified when I took the towel off and discovered it didn't turn my hair Blonde Bombshell like the box promised.

"By who?" Kevin asks as he pushes his way into my office, sans invitation.

"Zendaya. Ariana Grande. Various Kardashians."

I flick my wrist like I have any idea what I'm talking about but it's a ruse.

In my google search to figure out how to fix my mistake, I discovered two things. One, any more treatment would probably make my hair fall out and two, I got lucky because this color is really stylish. Which didn't make me feel that much better because I'm not a fashionista at all, but at least no one walking down the street has looked at me like I came straight from the circus. And if Kevin decides to google it later, he'll see I'm not wrong.

"What are you doing here, Kevin?" I ask, hoping to distract him from any more talk about my hair.

Misinterpreting my question as an invitation to stay awhile, Kevin sits in the chair across from my desk and leans back, adjusting the badge on his lanyard.

As an inspector for the health department, Kevin makes his rounds to the various salons in the area, making sure all the supplies are stored appropriately and cleaning records are kept. Once he had to follow up on a complaint about a local nail salon not properly cleaning their tools which led to an outbreak of a nasty toe fungus. He was really excited about that project. All I learned is I prefer to do my own pedicures.

"I got done with my last inspection early so I thought I'd come check on you before I go to lunch. See how you're doing since… well, you know."

I smile shyly, appreciating that he still has some concern for me in spite of breaking, er, maybe just bruising my heart. "Thank you for asking but I'm fine."

"Are you sure? Because your hair…"

I bristle and pat my chignon again, a little miffed he brought it up again. "It's fashionable and the color many women pay hundreds of dollars to achieve."

Thankfully, he has the wherewithal to look regretful over his choice of words. "You're right. It's just going to take me some time to get used to."

He's not the only one, but in the interest of self-preservation, I keep that thought to myself.

"I really didn't mean to hurt you, Ellery. You're still my best friend."

My lips tilt up into a soft smile. This should be more painful than it is and I can't figure out why. Was he right all along? Would we be better off as friends? It's going to take some getting used to, but maybe once I get used to the new normal, we'll be okay.

I swallow down the lump that has suddenly caught in my throat. Regardless of where we end up, we still have a long history that feels oddly hard to let go of. "You're mine, too. We've been through so much together. It would be a shame to throw it all aside just because we didn't end up together. And who knows, maybe you'll miss me at some point and we'll still have our happily ever after."

His whole body language changes from the relaxed,

easy-going posture he's had since he walked in to stiff and on-edge. The vibe around him changes and I know I've touched on something he's trying to keep from me.

Out of nowhere, it hits me. I know what's happening.

Kevin broke up with me after seven years with no indication we had any problems. No fights. No big upcoming life decisions. No issues with each other's parents. Just suddenly one day, it was over.

And as soon as the deed was done, he had dinner plans. Plans he had made knowing I would be out of the picture.

Tilting my head to the side, I look at Kevin as he shifts in his seat like he knows I've figured something out.

"Kevin," I say quietly, not sure if I'm holding back anger or tears. "Who did you go to dinner with the other night?"

Like a deer in the headlights, his eyes widen. It's just for a second, but I see it.

"What?" he croaks out.

"After we broke up. You told me you had dinner plans. That's why you were dressed up. Who did you eat with after breaking my heart?"

I'm figuring out that is a gross exaggeration of how the situation felt to me but now that circumstances seem to be changing, I'm not sure I care to tone it down.

Kevin swallows hard looking terrified that I'm about to jump over this desk and strangle him. I'd never do that, though. I like my job. I like being seen as a professional. I'm up for a promotion. I wouldn't waste all that on an emotional breakdown.

The longer he delays, the higher a huge red flag goes up in my head. After seven years, maybe Kevin and I didn't really know each other at all. Or maybe I just didn't know him.

"I, uh…" he stumbles and fidgets with his badge. A badge I suddenly find irritating. A small man's way of finding power. "I had a blind date."

It feels like the bottom drops out beneath me, but I make sure not to show it.

"Your friends thought it was a good idea to set you up on a blind date when you had a girlfriend?"

He runs his hands down his jeans. They're probably clammy all of a sudden from him fessing up to this mess. "Uh… my friends didn't set me up."

"Who did?"

He pauses before dropping the bombshell I didn't see coming.

"My mother."

I fall back in my chair, stunned. His mother. The woman I thought loved me and was looking forward to me being her daughter-in-law. The woman I looked up to as a business professional. *My boss.*

"That's, uh, why she wanted me to come check on you."

My head whips over to look at him again as he unknowingly sticks his foot in his mouth.

"She wanted to make sure you weren't having any issues with work or whatever since we broke up."

I hold my hands out to stop him as the pieces of the puzzle come together "Wait. Let me make sure I understand this." I lean forward holding eye contact so he can't lie his way out of this. I've always been able to read him by looking directly into his eyes. "Your mother, who has hosted me at every holiday for the last seven years, set you up with someone else before we broke up."

"Technically we were broken up when I took her to dinner."

"By thirty seconds. And then your mother sends you in here to check on me, not because she's concerned about my well-being but because she wants to make sure our breakup, that she orchestrated, isn't negatively affecting my ability to do my job."

Kevin clears his throat uncomfortably. "She said the Smithers account is pretty important."

I blink a few times, floored by the entire situation and wanting to kick myself. All the sacrifices I made. All the dreams I gave up. All the, the hairstyles I could have tried. But no. My life revolved around Kevin and his family. What would make them happy. What would make them comfortable. What would make them approve.

I have been Kevin's best friend for seven years, but he's never been mine. I've been a comfort to him, like a security blanket that's always there to make him feel better. He never loved me as anything more than a child's assurance.

Flabbergasted, I huff out a small laugh. "Get out of my office."

My words are resolved, with no hint of malice. I don't have the energy to be angry. Later. Later I'll let myself feel everything, but not now. Not in front of the man whose betrayal runs deeper than I could ever imagine.

He stands, still looking unsure. "I'm really sorry Ellery."

Turning my gaze on him, I give him more truth than I ever thought I was capable of.

"I don't believe you. Please don't check on me again."

He stands frozen, obviously uncomfortable with my dismissal.

Good. He needs to be uncomfortable. He probably also needs to rot somewhere but I refuse to go that far. I may be angry. I may be hurt. I may feel these deep wounds for a long time. But I'm still *me*. And I refuse to change the kindness I try to extend just because I was a pawn for all those years.

Finally, he turns and walks out the door. For the first time, I hope I never see him again.

SIX

Liam

Piiiiing!

I hate that sound. Especially first thing in the morning when I'm the only one here and there isn't a goalie stopping my shots from getting where they should be—in the net, not bouncing off the damn goalposts from shitty aim.

Rotating my arm, I grimace as the pain flares through my shoulder.

"Don't be a pussy, Tremblay," I mutter to myself and swing again. This time the puck ends up where I want, but slower than it should.

I shake my head, cursing this fucking shoulder for still giving me grief. It's a stupid injury. Hell, it's not even an injury. It's more like an old man's body breaking down and I don't have time for that.

I'm thirty-one years old for shit's sake. I'm not old by anyone's standards. Anyone except everyone in the hockey arena. And that's the part that pisses me off. This is what could force me into retirement. I wouldn't be the first one. The average age of calling it quits is just under thirty, but I wanted to be the exception to the rule. I wanted to be the next Zdeno Chara who is still playing in his forties. Instead, I may very well be like everyone else.

Thwack!

My stick slams the puck into the net and once again, a shooting pain runs through my shoulder.

"You gotta swing faster than that if you wanna make it back to the first line."

I didn't hear anyone come in, but that's not unusual. Maintenance staff and various administrators sometimes swing through the arena on their way to work or just to let the chill of the icy room invigorate them, so I don't notice the sound of footsteps anymore. Should have known he would find me.

"Why do you think I'm out here so early?" I quip back at my coach. I was hoping to avoid him before anyone else shows up to get some practice time in but it seems I'm out of luck these days in more ways than one.

We both watch as I whack at the puck again, still slower than I'd like but at least it goes where I want. Unlike this conversation.

"I'd say you're avoiding getting inside the MRI machine to figure out what's going on with that bum shoulder."

"Fucking Harry," I complain under my breath as I line up my shot again. But of course, Coach hears me.

"Don't blame this one on the trainer," Couch shouts. "You think he's the only one who can tell you're favoring it? I've got eyes. And you're so busy trying to prove you're not an old man, you're letting this linger. It's catching up to you."

Knowing this conversation is a long time coming,

I give up and skate over to the side, pulling my gloves off and using the bottom of my long-sleeve dry-fit shirt to wipe the sweat off my brow.

"You're the coach. Of course, you notice. It's your job to see things like that."

He harumphs. "And you're the player. It's your job to make sure your body is in tip-top shape instead of this pansy-ass avoidance bullshit you've got going on."

"It's not avoidance."

"Really? Then what is it?"

"It's no big deal. We play with injuries all the time. I'm working through the pain."

He nods slowly but I'm not convinced it's in agreement. "Okay. I'll bite. Let's say it is no big deal. Then you've got a big problem because you're slowing down rapidly. We'll be forcing you into retirement sooner rather than later at this rate."

I clench my jaw. "Is that a threat?"

"Not even close. It's the reality of the situation."

I look out on the ice where I've spent the last six years of my life. I love this place and I'm terrified it's all going away. Men in their sixties freak out about leaving the job they've had most of their lives. I'm half that age.

"What would I even do with the next seventy years of my life if I don't come here?" I mutter, maybe more to myself than him.

He shrugs. "Coach. Sit on your ass and play the stock market. Find a nice woman and settle down. There are a lot of options."

Thoughts of a dark-haired beauty flit through my brain. The idea of starting something with Ellery that could lead to a long-term relationship sounds pretty appealing. She intrigued me the other night. But that doesn't mean I can envision taking care of her, providing for her, without my job. It's what makes me *me*.

"Let's flip the situation though," Coach continues. "Say this is a big deal like I think it is and that your shoulder has an injury that needs some attention. You get it fixed, you get back to it, and you get back up to par."

I look away, realizing how simple it sounds when he says it that way. So why am I frozen in place? Why can't I seem to do anything about it?

"I get it. You're afraid this is the end of the road. Hockey is a short-lived sport and you've already outlived everyone else. You're having the athletic version of a mid-life crisis. You wouldn't be the first one. Problem is, if you don't stop being a pussy and get this taken care of, I guarantee your career is over. If this is fixable, at least you have a shot. It's your choice on how you want to handle this."

Leave it to Coach to lay it on the line for me.

"I'll leave you to it since I'll never harp on a player for getting in some extra practice, even if he is being an idiot." He turns to leave, still calling out orders. "But get your ass in that machine before you're out of time and not even surgery can fix it."

Pulling my gloves back on, I get back on the line and continue working on my shot. Every twinge of pain I feel, every tweak, and his words come back to me.

"If it's surgical at least you have a shot."
Thwack!
It's your choice on how you want to handle this.
Thwack!
If you don't stop being a pussy and get this taken care of, I guarantee your career is over.
Thwack!
I run out of pucks the same time I run out of steam. I

hate that he's right. I'm being a pussy because I'm scared of the results. I feel like climbing in that machine is the athletic equivalent of walking to my own execution. But I can't keep going like this. Even getting good sleep is harder since I'm waking up to the pain more and no amount of ibuprofen is taking the edge off anymore.

Resigned and finally, with enough nerve, I leave the arena and head to the locker room. If I know Coach, Harry is probably waiting for me already.

• • •

Just like I thought, Harry had already called the orthopedic surgeon the team has on staff. By eight in the morning, I was in the lobby of his office, waiting to be called. By nine, it was all over.

Now I'm lying on the examination table, legs dangling over the side, fingers laced together on my chest as I wait for the results and try not to worry what direction my life is about to take. Perks of the job—results that take everyone else a day to get back takes us a couple of hours tops.

My eyes closed, I concentrate on my breathing and let my thoughts drift to Ellery. Except for being worried about my shoulder, I haven't stopped thinking about her since the night we met. She looked so sad when she walked in, but it was quickly replaced with this bubbly personality that drew me in. Yes, she was heading towards hammered, but it was more than that.

She had this innocence about her. Maybe it was a bit of naivete and lack of experience, too. But also a bit like she prefers to see the good things in life. Obviously, living with rose-colored glasses on didn't help with her boyfriend situation. That guy sounds like a dick. But on her it was refreshing. She isn't jaded by the world. I liked it.

I also liked her candor when she got a little alcohol in her. Even thinking about how she said my name makes me laugh to myself.

"Liiiiiiiam."

She even wrote it in a text. A text I kept but haven't responded to yet. I will. I'm just waiting for her to settle into her newfound singleness first. At least that's the excuse I'm giving myself. Really, I'm hoping to run into her at the bar again so I can get to know her better before full out pursuing her.

I hear the door open and Dr. Fantasma chuckle.

"Those beds are quite comfortable in a pinch, aren't they?"

Sitting up, I run my hand down my face. "I've slept on worse."

"You're reminding me of my residency," he says as he quickly washes his hands. In his early fifties but still sporting a full head of dark hair, Dr. Fantasma has the confidence of a man who knows he's good at his job. A little on the quirky side, he's quick with his assessments and always has a plan of action ready. That's probably why the team uses him for anything orthopedic. "Even an empty exam table is like sleeping on a cloud when you're in the middle of back-to-back twenty-four-hour shifts."

"I can imagine."

The good doctor pulls up a chair and sits in front of a computer off to the side. "Don't even try. I'm glad those days are over. I wouldn't want to pull a shift like that at this age. Probably why you don't see many older people tackling medical school. The residency would kill them."

Dr. Fantasma clicks a few keys on the keyboard in front of him and the monitor lights up. A few more clicks and what appears to be my scans show up.

"Hmmm," he says as he looks at them, clicking through multiple screens and zooming in and out while I impatiently wait for his conclusion about my fate.

My foot begins to wiggle without my permission from the pent-up energy I feel. He could send me off to some physical therapy or he could tell me to hang up my skates. His face is so unexpressive I have absolutely no idea what he's going to say.

Picking up a pen, he points at a spot on the screen. "Do you see this part right here?"

"That white spot? Yeah."

"Looks like you have an acromioclavicular joint injury."

I breathe a sigh of relief. AC injuries are common in my chosen profession, so I've seen the treatments done on other people before. I've just never felt one before so I assumed it was a rotator cuff which is much more challenging. This is good news. It's really good.

"So what—I get a referral to PT or something?"

"Mmmm…"

The smile falls from my face. I don't like the tone in that "mmm."

He clicks to another screen and leans in closer. "It's not just an injury, Liam. It's a pretty significant tear."

"What does that mean? I'm benched for a couple of weeks?"

Dr. Fantasma swivels the chair around and interlaces his fingers, placing them on one crossed knee. "I hate to be the bearer of bad news, but we're going to have to fix it surgically."

"Shit." My head drops as disappointment runs through me. Surgery means being out for weeks.

"It's not all bad," Dr. Fantasma says in his normal even

tone. "It's a relatively easy surgery so you won't have to stay in the hospital. In and out the same day."

"But how long until I'm back on the ice."

"Oh, well that's a different story." He says it like he forgot about that part. Odd coming from the team orthopedic surgeon, but he is one of the best so I guess bedside manner isn't a big deal. "Obviously, we'll know more after surgery but with a tear this size, I'm guesstimating about twelve weeks."

My jaw drops. "Twelve weeks? There's no way I can be out that long."

He bobbles his head and I know whatever he's about to say isn't good. "That's assuming all goes well and you follow all the instructions carefully. Push it too quickly and we'll be back where we started. One body-check, one fall on that shoulder, and you'll never be the same again."

I run my hand down my face, disappointment coursing through me. How will I get back up to speed if I'm out for several months? The only saving grace is we're still three months away from the beginning of the season, but still. That doesn't give me much time to get back into shape without missing the whole season.

"Okay," I finally concede. "Let's just get me into physical therapy as soon as possible. I'll be fine pushing through the post-surgery pain. Maybe I'll get lucky and will be cleared to play by the start of the season."

Dr. Fantasma picks up a folded sheet of paper and begins reading through it. "Sounds like a solid plan. Now let's get your surgery scheduled so we can get this ball rolling."

SEVEN

Ellery

The same dark SUVs are in the parking lot as I pull in again. Only this time there's no rain forcing me here. I'm meeting some old friends.

Even as I exit the car, I can't help feeling a bit excited. Girls don't usually include me in their get-togethers. They never have. Actually, boys never do either. I'm not sure if it's because I'm not as experienced as them in, well, anything, or if there's something wrong with me. Maybe I hold myself back. Like I just don't put in enough reciprocal effort myself to keep a relationship going thinking maybe they don't really want me there. But that is all about to change.

I always liked Lauren. She was bold and confident. She never treated me like an oddball. I'm excited to get to know her again and hope we hit it off. I wouldn't mind being brought back into her fold. Her entire group of friends was always so loyal to each other. I've always wanted to be cared for like that.

Pulling open the door, I walk through and glance

around the room. I barely spot Lauren before my eyes dart away and lock on the one person I wasn't expecting to see but should have—Liam.

His gaze locks on mine and I'm frozen in place, not sure what to do with myself. Do I approach him and apologize for my inappropriate behavior? Do I ignore him, knowing he probably never wants to speak to me again? I have no idea what the best course of action is for this situation.

A female voice cuts through my thoughts and the decision is made for me.

"Ellery!" Lauren squeals and runs over, enveloping me in a huge hug. It's completely unexpected but not at all unwelcome as I hug her back. "How are you?" She pulls back and runs a lock of my hair through her fingers. "Ohmygod your hair!"

I feel myself blush at my screw-up. "It's really bad, isn't it?"

Her eyes widen temporarily. "Bad? No way. It's gorgeous!"

Relief runs through me now that she's confirmed I was right and, in some circles, this is considered trendy. When I spouted that mess off to Kevin I wasn't totally sure I knew what I was talking about. But Lauren doesn't mince words. She would tell me if the color looked terrible.

Lacing her arm through mine, she drags me to the bar where Kiersten is pouring drinks alongside a younger blonde woman.

"I'm so glad you said that," I admit, feeling my nerves settle as I talk to my old friend. It's been years since we've seen each other and she's acting like nothing has changed between us. "I was trying for blonde and I don't know if I messed up the bleach or something, but this is what happened."

We slide onto the stools as we chat.

"You did that at home on accident?" Lauren runs her fingers through my hair again. "People pay good money for that color these days."

I scrunch my nose. "You don't think it looks weird?"

"Not at all."

Kiersten approaches, a smile on her face. "I'm so glad you made it, Ellery. You look great. You drinking again tonight?"

I feel a blush creep up my face at the reminder of what happened last time I was here.

"Maybe I need to stick with soft drinks this time since I am obviously a lightweight."

She gives me an amused look. "You sure? You are actually a really fun drunk. Not everyone is, and I would know."

I nod. "I'm sure. Getting my car back the next morning before work was a pain. I'd rather avoid that again if I can."

"Sure thing." Kiersten spouts off all my options and I order a Dr. Pepper, because you can't reside in Texas and not drink it regularly. It's practically a requirement to live here.

Lauren orders a Shiner, another Texas staple, and turns back to me. "You know what would make you feel better about your hair?"

"If I rewound the clock and talked myself out of trying something new?"

She giggles and slaps my leg lightly. "No. You need makeup that matches."

Makeup that matches? What does that even mean? Purple eyeshadow?

I don't have to ask the question. She can see the confusion written all over my face.

"Your hair is on point but your makeup just needs a little funk to it."

"I still have no idea what that means."

"Kiersten," Lauren says just as our bartending friend drops off our drinks. "Don't you think Ellery could use a bit of an update on her makeup to pull this whole style together?"

Kiersten cocks her head and looks at me critically for a second. "A winged eyeliner would look fabulous on you."

"You mean with the…" my hands wave around my face as I try to describe what I'm thinking but being too flustered to succeed. "… the wingy and the… the black and the…"

Both my friends, laugh. Or are they acquaintances at this point? Regardless, they both start laughing at how flabbergasted I am.

"Relax." Lauren puts her hand on my forearm, probably trying to calm me down. "We'll do a makeover this weekend. It'll be fun."

"Nooooooo, nonononono." I take a quick sip of my drink hoping to relieve my suddenly dry mouth. "My office is very conservative. They wouldn't go for it at all."

Lauren cocks her head at me. "Lavender hair is okay but a little eyeliner is too much?"

I can feel my eyes widen as I realize she's right. "Because the hair was an accident?" I squeak out.

"I like her," Kiersten says to Lauren. "I forgot how funny she is. Where's Annika anyway?"

"She said she wasn't feeling well. That's probably code for Jaxon is home and they need some alone time." The two of them laugh at a joke I don't quite understand. I get the gist of it, but I'm pretty sure I'm missing something that makes the quip funny.

Just then, the blonde bartender sets a tray in front of Kiersten and begins placing drinks on it. "Sorry to break up girls' night but the table full of gentlemen is getting thirsty."

Without skipping a beat, Kiersten slides under the bar and comes out on our side. "Duty calls, ladies. Let Nicole know if you need anything if I'm not back for a while." She balances the now full tray on one shoulder, a very impressive feat, and walks away.

"I can't believe you guys have stayed friends all these years." If I sound like I'm in awe, it's because I am. I've never had a friendship last after whatever event threw us together in the first place was over. Unless you count Kevin and at this point, I'm not sure I can anymore.

Lauren shrugs like it's no big deal. "She's my person. Well, Heath is my person. But Kiersten is a close second. Plus, I have to stick around for Carson. He's the best."

"Is that the baby?"

She nods, an adoring smile on her face. "He's not a baby anymore. That boy is going into first grade this coming year and is already doing triple-digit addition."

I don't know what that means in relationship to his age, but I pretend to be impressed anyway.

"It's so great that you guys have each other."

Lauren leans so far onto the counter, she's practically laying on it, resting her chin on her arm. "You don't have that?"

I glance down at my drink, suddenly ashamed to make eye contact. "I thought I did. Turns out I *was* the friend but I didn't actually *have* a friend."

"Kevin, huh?"

She says it so gently, it almost hurts worse than if she'd

just come out and say she thinks he's a jerk and she's always hated him or something.

"That's what happened to my hair. I guess it was like a post-break-up decision to go blonde. I don't really understand why I did it."

"Same reason we all do it when our heart is bleeding. It gives us some distance from the life we had and pushes us to the life we're moving toward."

I fidget with my straw, thinking about what she said. It's going to take a heck of a lot more than a new hair color to get enough distance from that situation.

Lauren nudges my shoulder. "Did it work? The radical change?"

I shake my head. "Not even close."

She spins my stool so I'm forced to face her. "Then let me do your makeup. It'll be fun to feel like a new person for the day. We can do it Saturday afternoon and then come back here to try it out and see what total strangers think."

I huff a laugh. "That's what I'm supposed to be doing now? Caring what strangers think?"

"You know what I mean." She pulls up an app on her phone and begins scrolling. "I'm not talking about drag makeup. Just something complementary to your new hair. Something like this."

She turns the phone to show me a picture. The woman, probably a model, looks glamourous with a nude lip and smoky eye. Her hair color is similar to mine, although obviously done by a professional. Even I have to admit, she looks amazing.

Taking the phone from Lauren, I enlarge the picture to get a better look at some of the detail. "I'm not that good with makeup. You really think I can do this?"

"Absolutely. You'll be stunning."

"I think she looks beautiful exactly as she is."

My eyes widen at the deep voice behind me.

Liam.

I may have only met him once, and I may have been inebriated, but I'll never forget the deep timbre of his voice.

Lauren doesn't even bother trying to hide her reaction to his approach, making sure I'm fully aware that she approves of this turn of events.

Grabbing her beer, she slides off the stool and lies through her teeth. "I think I hear Kiersten calling me. I'll see you two later."

I watch as she saunters off, determined to avoid eye contact with the man I made a fool out of myself in front of the other day. But then he leans in and whispers in my ear.

"I really like your hair."

My head moves before I can stop it, and I'm suddenly looking into his eyes, excited to see approval in them.

"You do?"

He nods. "It's different than before, but you kind of look like a fairy."

"I'm honestly not sure if that's a good or bad thing."

He shrugs. "It's just a thing. But for some reason, it seems to suit you." Reaching over, he pulls a lock through his fingers. "And I really like it out of that bun thingy."

"You do?" I whisper, captivated by his voice, his words. Even his scent. He smells like soap and mint and ice. Which doesn't make sense to me at all, but it's true. He reminds me of that fresh smell after it snows. I've only experienced it once when I went skiing but I'll never forget that scent.

Putting some distance between us, he takes a deep breath and I wonder if he's as affected by me as I am by him. Doubtful. I'm Ellery McIlroy. I don't attract super-hot men. I don't attract any men, actually. Yet here he is so that has to mean something, right?

"I like that you're allowing yourself to let loose a little. Based on our conversation the other night, I don't think you do that enough."

I blush, reminded of how forward I was with him. "I'm sorry if I made you uncomfortable. I'm not usually so flirty."

When he smiles at me, I'm blasted with heat through my entire body. He's so freaking attractive. Why is he talking to me? Wouldn't he rather hit on the blonde bartender? She's gorgeous.

"You didn't make me uncomfortable."

"Are you sure?"

He nods and relief runs through me. It's not that I'm terribly worried about what other people think of me. I just don't like doing things that put people in awkward situations.

"You were really cute. Especially when you said my name."

His lips quirk up on the side and I'm reminded of exactly how flirty I was.

"Oh god," I groan, a hand over my face.

"Liiiiiiiam," he says, obviously imitating me. "It was even better when it came through by text."

"I still can't believe I did that."

"Relax." He nudges my shoulder with his gently. "It was a fun night. I needed it. It'd been a really crappy day so I appreciate that you changed my mood."

"You'd had a crappy day, too?"

"Maybe not as crappy as yours, but yeah."

I fidget with my straw, determined to enjoy Liam's company while he's still interested.

"Care to tell me about it?"

His expression changes, darkens a bit. "It's no big deal."

"Doesn't look like it's no big deal." He doesn't respond and for some reason, I feel the need to push him a little. "I told you all about my crappy day. It's your turn to share. Fair is fair, ya know."

He turns back to me, leaning his big body against the counter, his bicep straining the sleeve of his shirt. He looks at me then takes a deep breath.

"I play hockey for a living."

I can tell by the guarded expression on his face that I reacted with surprise, even if I didn't intend to.

"It's not a big deal. It's just a job like anyone else's," he says sheepishly, likely trying to stop any fangirl action before it starts. Not that I would do that.

"Well, not really, but I understand what you mean," I say. "I didn't mean to react. I've just never met a professional hockey player before."

"But you've met other professional athletes?"

"I know Lauren's boyfriend, Heath. He plays football still, right? Wait. That was dumb. Not all pro athletes know each other." I shake off my embarrassment but Liam just chuckles.

"In this case, I actually do know Heath. We have the same agent."

"Oh. Small world. Anyway, sorry. Continue with your crappy day."

"Right. I've been having some pain in my shoulder and was kind of in avoidance mode the day we met. That's why I was in a bad mood. Until we started talking, that is."

With just those two sentences, I feel a strange sort of confidence. I helped this man, this very attractive, very successful if he's a pro athlete, very interesting man have a better day. I'm not used to this kind of compliment. But it makes me feel good. Like maybe I'm not as forgettable as I've always believed.

Something sparks in me. A desire to take life by the horns and put myself out there more. If two drinks at a bar can help this incredible man feel better, what have I been missing out on by holding back on trying new things or exploring who I am?

I know it's not just this conversation. It's also the gaping hole Kevin left. Not with his sudden breakup speech, but the realization that trying to be someone I might not actually be wasn't good enough for him, or his mother even. So why am I holding myself back from experiencing life? Because I'm worried about losing relationships that are only surface level anyway? Where has that gotten me?

Sitting in a bar, hoping to rekindle old friendships because I have none, finally understanding that I've got more life to live than I know what to do with. But I have this feeling in my gut that Liam knows how. And that he will be willing to show me.

Feeling a sudden burst of confidence, I lean in and place my hand on his thigh. I'm not sure if I'm being seductive or supportive but I'm not afraid to try and find out this time.

"How is your shoulder feeling now?"

Liam's brow raises and he looks down at my hand. His nostrils flare for just a split second, as if he's trying to maintain some form of control. I still don't know if I'm being flirty or crossing some unwritten line, but he makes no move to push my hand away so I take that as a good sign.

"It uh…" he clears his throat and I feel so powerful by rendering him speechless. Is this what women mean when they say they feel empowered? "It still hurts like a bitch. Have to have surgery next week to fix it."

I remove my hand and he shakes his head just slightly.

"I'm sorry. That must be really scary."

"Not scary as much as frustrating. I'll be out for at least twelve weeks which is messing with my brain, I think."

"I get that. Nothing like thinking you're set at your job and suddenly a wrench is thrown in it and you no longer know where you stand."

"You do get it."

"I work for my ex-boyfriend's mother, remember?" I shift in myself, too embarrassed to look at him while I tell him the whole truth. "Turns out she's the one who set him up with the girl he took out to dinner an hour after he broke up with me."

"Oh, now that is some shit right there."

"Yep. But it opened my eyes to a few things."

"Really? Like what?"

"Like I wasted a lot of years trying to be something that I might not actually be, trying to fit into that world. But what if I'm not that person? What if I'm actually someone completely different and I just don't know it because I've never explored any other side of me?"

"I'd say you're doing a good job figuring it out already." He touches my hair again and it reminds me I can take chances. There is nothing stopping me. The world is my oyster or however the saying goes, I just have to go for it.

My heart beating rapidly, I make a decision I hope I won't regret tomorrow. Somehow, though, I don't think I will.

"Can I ask you a question? And if it's totally inappropriate, or you don't want to just say so and I'll be fine."

He downs the last of his drink and turns to me. "Shoot."

"Will you go home with me for the night?"

I purposely throw the words out in a rush, not because I think I'll change my mind, but because I'm afraid I'd lose my nerve otherwise.

Liam just looks at me, probably trying to gather his thoughts. I know what his hesitation is, so I don't allow him to even say it.

"I know I was drunk the other night when I first propositioned you, and you were right to decline. I would have woken up the next morning with regrets. But that's why I'm asking you now, when I'm one hundred percent sober—because looking back on the last decade of my life, I've never taken the time to explore who I am. What I like to do. Who I am as a person or a woman and I want to change that. It started with the hair, but there's more to life than just the vanity part, you know? I've never had a one-night stand and I know that's not a bad thing, but what if it turns out I like sex? What if I like more than missionary position and, there are other things, too? How will I ever know if I don't take the time to learn?"

Liam swallows hard, this voice coming out husky and deep. "And you think I'm the one to show you all that?"

I shrug, my lips tilted up in a smirk. "I don't know. But I think you'll be respectful and kind and if it turns out I'm not a one-night stand kind of girl, you won't be the guy to treat me like dirt after the fact."

I don't know how I am so sure of his character. Maybe it's because Kiersten trusted him to get me into an Uber. Maybe it's because he turned down a drunk woman who threw herself at him. Maybe it's because Lauren so quickly left us alone and Lauren never used to leave us alone with men she didn't trust in public. Girl code and all that.

But somehow, I know deep down inside that Liam is one of the good ones.

"I would never disrespect a woman like that."

"We've only met a couple of times, but if I trust anyone with treating me with respect, no matter what the outcome, it's you."

Gesturing to get the bartender's attention, he tosses his credit card on the counter.

"Are you absolutely sure you want to do this?"

Nervous excitement runs through me. Even if I wanted to back out, I wouldn't. Just the possibility of having one night with a man like Liam has me feeling eager to get back to my place. It's as if all these possibilities of who I am and who I might be have been awakened and a night of passion is the way I'm going to figure out the key to it all.

"I've never been more sure in my life," I whisper.

He blinks once, a lusty haze on his face. Reaching out, he runs the back of his finger down my cheek. It leaves a trail of burning nerve endings in its wake. "If you change your mind, all you have to do is say so."

"Which is exactly why I won't."

I know with everything in me, this will be a turning point in my life. Forget my car. Maybe trying new things isn't a bad idea after all.

EIGHT

Liam

The air in my truck is thick with sexual tension. Ever since Ellery propositioned me the first time, fantasies of what could happen have run through my mind regularly. I have had to lean against my shower wall more than once after giving myself a mind-blowing orgasm to thoughts of what she looks like when she comes. But that was nothing compared to just being in this car with her, knowing what's coming.

But I have to be sure. I don't want to see the light dim in Ellery's eyes. I won't be responsible for that. I'd rather use my hand in the shower for the rest of my life than take away the aura around her. If she hasn't thought this through, if she even suspects she will have regrets, she's not ready for this.

"I know I sound like a broken record but I have to be absolutely sure this is what you want. Not that you can't make your own choices. You just don't strike me as a rebound girl."

"Turn right there." She points to the road ahead.

"That's the thing. I don't really know what kind of girl I am. I've spent seven years trying to be someone else's idea of appropriate. What if I'm not actually her? What if I'm a closet nympho and I don't even know it because I've never had the chance to find out?"

I choke back nervous laughter. "I'd say that ex-boyfriend wasn't doing it right in the first place if that's the case."

"I don't know if he was doing it right. Or wrong. Or even mediocre." She turns to me, lust in her eyes and I know this is definitely happening. "I just want the chance to find out. About myself. About the things my body likes and doesn't like." She licks her bottom lip and I already know whatever she's about to say is going to make me groan. "And I want to find those things out with you."

Yep. I'm done for.

Pulling into the parking lot she guides me to, I throw the truck in park. Reaching over, I grab her by the back of the neck and gently pull her to me, sealing our lips together. She squeaks in surprise as my tongue invades her mouth and the sound makes my dick stand up at attention. There's no reason to go slow. The feel of her, the taste of her, the smell of her makes it impossible for me to take my time anyway. At least not in the cab of my truck. I want more, need more. From the way her hands grasp at my shoulders, I know she feels the same way.

Reluctantly, I pull away, but hopefully not for long.

"I will come upstairs with you. I will make you come so hard you see stars. And then I'll do it again and again, just to help you find out more about your body than you've ever known." She gasps at my words. "But you have to be absolutely sure. I know I keep saying it, but I will stop right here and now if there is even a question of you getting hurt once it's over."

Her wide eyes blink just once as she focuses on my words. "Oh wow. I never knew chivalry could be so sexy."

"It's not chivalry. It's human decency."

"Call it whatever you want. But if you don't take me upstairs and ravage me like I've read about in those Regency romances, I will never forgive you."

I smile at her inability to control her hormones. It makes me pissed off that whoever this Kevin guy is apparently gave her the bare minimum of a relationship. Ellery deserves better than that.

I don't know where the situation between us is going, but I do know it's about to be upstairs in her bedroom.

"Come on."

I slide Ellery across the seat, lifting her out on my side of the truck simply so I don't have to stop touching her.

Tangling her fingers with mine, she pulls me toward the staircase.

The apartment complex is a little on the older side but kept up nicely. Fresh paint, fresh landscaping, looks freshly power washed. It's a nice neighborhood, which I'm glad for. Someone like Ellery should always live in a place that is safe and well maintained.

Her green door has a festive wreath with American flags all over it, announcing the July 4th holiday which is already over. I chuckle to myself. It seems Ellery may be a lover of holiday decorating. I like knowing that about her.

We're blasted with cool air conditioning when she finally pushes her door open, and the hairs on my arms stand on end. I'm not sure if it's the change in temperature or anticipation of what's coming.

Ellery clears her throat, leaning back against the now closed door, hands behind her. "So. This is my place."

"It's nice," I reply because what else is there to say? It looks like any other apartment I've been in—living room, kitchen, dining area. The furniture touches are obviously all hers, with a comfortable, homey vibe. But I'm not interested in discussing her decorating skills.

Sensing her nervousness, I approach, pressing both hands against the door behind her, caging her tiny body in. I knew she was short, but until this moment, I didn't realize how much. I could pick her up and toss her in the air.

Maybe later, but for now, I reach down and pick her up by her thighs, pushing her skirt out of the way, and wrap both legs around my waist. She gasps.

"That's better," I remark now that we're at eye level without me having to crouch over.

"I wasn't expecting that."

"But did you like it?"

She thinks for a second before a smile crosses her face. "I did. It was very alpha male of you."

This girl and the random things she says. I like it. I also like that she's so interested in trying new things. I can't wait to find out what else she wants to try.

With no more patience, I take her lips in a searing kiss. It's not gentle. It's harsh and demanding, and she matches my tongue stroke for stroke. Her hands begin moving over my body, touching everywhere she can reach, clawing at my shirt. Pulling back, I use one hand to hold her up, the other to tug it over my head, careful when my shoulder tweaks.

She sighs when her eyes land on my naked chest. I've never had that reaction from a woman before, but it's not unwelcome. It's more than appreciated when she begins nibbling on my neck, down to my collarbone. She is as amped up as I am and I'm ready to show her things she never knew her body could do.

"This is all about you, babe," I remind her, watching as her tongue snakes out to intertwine small licks with tiny bites and sucks on my chest. It's driving me wild. "We have all night so we can start here. Or we can go straight for the bed. It's your call."

"Bed. I want room for us to roll around if we want."

My eyes roll into the back of my head. "Fuck, you are going to kill me, aren't you?"

"Only if you teach me how."

A growl rumbles from deep in my throat. "You better show me where the bed is or I'm going to take you right against this wall."

Her eyes widen. "You can really do that? I've never done that. Maybe I want that instead."

I grind into her and she gasps in response. Nuzzling into her neck, I begin sucking, licking, nipping at a spot behind her ear that makes her groan.

"Yeah, I want it like this first," she pants, and I don't miss the word "first". I have plans for all kinds of things I can show her "second" and "third" and "fourth". "Do you have a condom?"

Dammit. "Not on me. Do we need to stick with oral tonight?"

Ellery whimpers and then pushes me away, jumping down onto the floor. "Don't move from this spot."

She takes off at a solid jog into what I assume is her bedroom. Mere seconds later, she emerges with a large box in her hands. "I got the variety pack, well, for variety. So, which one do you want?"

Her over-preparedness makes me laugh if I don't think too hard about who she was originally trying to have variety with. I grab one of the *ribbed for her pleasure* condoms knowing it'll have some extra room for me since I'm a little larger than the average man. Proportional to my body type and all that.

As soon as it's in my hand she drops the box and jumps back in my arms, not holding back as she kisses me deeply, her hands reaching for whatever naked skin she can find.

My hands push up her thighs, moving her skirt out of the way again so I can have access between her legs. Sliding up the back of her thighs, I move her panties out of the way, and lightly brush her opening with my finger. She gasps and I know that's my cue to keep going.

Confident that she's secure against the wall and not going anywhere, I reach one hand around and slip my finger insider her. Ellery groans, her mouth still touching mine, but too sidetracked to do anything more than breathe as I thrust in and out, add another finger, and bring her to the brink of orgasm before slowing down.

Annoyed by her panties but pleased to realize they're mostly made of lace, I force my fingers through the material and pull as hard as I can, careful to put all the pressure on my hands so I don't hurt her.

Ellery giggles. "Are you really ripping my panties off of me?"

"Ripping sounds way more delicate than what I'm doing. I'm shredding these puppies to get them out of my way."

"It's way faster and sexier when I read about it."

"I'm not worried about being sexy, I just need better access to that sweet spot right there." My thumb grazes over top of her again just as the offending material falls away. "That's better."

I explore for just a few seconds longer before my cock demands attention of his own. Balancing Ellery on my thighs, I quickly work the button and zipper of my jeans, sliding them down over my hips as far as I can without losing my balance.

Ellery keeps her gaze down, watching the reveal as she licks her lips. When I'm finally fully exposed, she wraps her tiny hand around me and I feel like I'm going to fall over from her touch.

"Wow. That's… bigger than I expected," she breathes, slowly stroking me, building up the fire inside me.

Ripping the condom packet open, I hand it to her. "You want to do the honors?"

Her hands shaking ever so slightly, she takes it from me and with expert precision, sheaths me quickly.

Both of us pant in anticipation of what's about to happen. Gripping Ellery by the hips, I lift her up and we watch as I slowly impale her on me. We groan in unison as inch by inch she slides down until she's fully seated on me and all remaining thought is lost from my brain.

Pushing her up against the wall again, I begin thrusting slowly, then circling my hips, then thrusting quickly, learning what her body responds to and what makes her the wettest. My body feels like it's on fire, both wanting to find my release quickly and wanting to take it slow so she can find hers more than once.

When her nails dig into my back, I know it's game on.

"Liam… oh my… oh please keep going. Faster or… something. I don't know. Just please, please keep doing that."

Sliding my arms under her legs I open her wider and pound into her, taking her with a passion I didn't know was inside me. I need her to come, need it, before I can even think of letting myself go.

"Take all of me, baby," I whisper in her ear. "Feel all of

me. Ride me and use me. This is just the beginning."

Ellery leans her head back against the wall and with a groan from deep within, she comes, igniting the spark that sets off my own orgasm. It races up my spine and slams into me, rendering me speechless with the force of its pleasure.

I come and I come and I come, until I feel like I'm wrung dry.

Ellery's small pants of breath make the hairs on the back of my neck tickle, but I have no desire to move. I could stay like this, inside her, up against this wall, forever.

This woman has fucking ruined me. And I never want to look back.

NINE
Ellery

Lauren is going to know I had sex with Liam. She's looking right at my face. I bet she can tell he gave me several orgasms in a row and even licked places that have never been licked before. She can tell. I'm sure of it.

"Why is your face turning red?" Lauren pulls the sponge back and cocks her head to look at me.

I'm sitting on an office chair she rolled into her giant elegant bathroom. I've never seen a tub that big, but I guess that's what happens when your live-in boyfriend is one of the hottest NFL players in the league.

"Are you blushing?"

"No," I blurt out faster than anyone who doesn't have a secret night of hot sex ever would.

"Aaaaahhhhhh," she singsongs with a knowing smile on her face and begins patting my forehead with whatever foundation she's been using again. "Does this have anything to do with you leaving the bar with Liam the other night?"

If it's possible to blush any harder, I'm sure I do. I also

deny, deny, deny.

"I didn't leave with him. I mean, I left. But like, not *leave* leave. Or anything. Because I don't do things like that…"

My words fizzle out quietly because I'm the worst liar in the world. We both know it.

Lauren, thankfully, doesn't have a judgmental bone in her body, nor has she ever felt ashamed of having sex, so she doesn't even stop applying my makeup before calling me out.

"Ellery, did you have super-hot sex with a super-hot guy and you're feeling a teensy bit guilty because the breakup is still in its infancy?"

I sigh, relieved she's always so nonchalant about things I struggle with. I really need to talk this out before I explode.

"Yes. But it's not because of Kevin."

"Then what has you feeling guilty?"

It's a struggle to put into words how I feel because I feel so much.

"Honestly, I'm not sure."

"Can I take a stab at it?" She pulls back, pinching my chin between her thumb and forefinger, turning my face this way and that. "Just tell me if I'm wrong."

"Okay."

Satisfied with her handy work, she nods and picks up an eye shadow pallet, beginning the process of blending a couple of colors on a small brush.

"I think you grew up with very conservative parents who were wonderful people and love you dearly, but who you never wanted to disappoint because of how much they love you. Somehow in the middle of always looking for their approval, you began to associate conservative Suzy

Homemaker, or in your case working Suzy Homemaker, as the type of woman you should be. Close your eyes." I comply and she continues to paint my face while she talks. "While there is nothing wrong with that particular kind of woman, in your case, it means you never had the chance to explore other parts of yourself, including your sexuality which is suddenly something you want to do. So currently you are at odds with the fact that the conservative version of perfection you always thought you were striving for may not actually be so perfect. Oh, and that maybe you happen to like sex with someone who likes having sex with you, too."

That about sums up all the jumbled feelings I've been having.

"How did you know?"

"Open." She shrugs as she inspects her handiwork again. "I think we all go through some version of it at some point." Satisfied that everything looks right, she nods once. "Close again."

"I'm not sure we all have this kind of existential crisis," I argue as I feel her draw a wet line above my lashes and all the way out to the side of my face. Oh boy. She's drawing practically to my hairline. This is going to be so bad, I already know it. "You never seemed to struggle with your sexuality. You've always been so confident in yourself."

Lauren laughs lightly. "Not as much as you think. I'm just a master of covering up my anxiety when I feel vulnerable. Only the closest people to me can see through my defenses."

My skin prickles at the reminder that I'm not one of those people. Not that I expect to be after half a decade of distance, but it still stinks to know I should have spent those years cultivating relationships and didn't.

"It even took Heath forever to get past that wall. Open." She takes one look at my face and smiles in delight. "Ohmygod I'm so good at this. I should have been a cosmetologist," she mutters more to herself than me. "Close one last time."

"I wish I could hide my emotions like you do. I feel like everyone always knows what I'm feeling and like they judge me for it. The girl who is always nervous and afraid. Who never has her own opinions. The pushover."

"I'm glad you show your insecurities. It's one of the things I like about you. All your emotions are genuine and real. And never once is it negative toward anyone else."

"Except maybe Kevin right now."

"Ah yes. The devil himself. What happened with him anyway?"

I try not to shrug, afraid I'll be poked in the eye with some kind of utensil. "I don't really know. He said things fizzled out."

"And you believe that?"

"I don't really know what to believe. Can I ask you a question?"

"Sure. But hold still. I want to get these lashes just right."

I hold my body as still as I can, only moving my mouth. "Did you ever like Kevin?"

She pauses and I know she's trying to censor her words. "I didn't *not* like Kevin. I just didn't trust him."

"Why?"

"Because of who his friends were. Because he didn't have a backbone. Because it's like he knew the right thing to do, but when it came time to choose, he followed the crowd even if they were wrong."

78

I think on her words and remember all the times in college his "friends" were jerks and he didn't do anything about it. He never participated, he just never told them to stop either. Like when his friend on the team, Conrad screwed Lauren, literally, Kevin just listened and laughed along with everyone else.

Or when his mom made me work tons of overtime a couple of years ago and then denied my request for an additional vacation day to go to my dad's seventieth birthday party because things were "just starting to get back to normal." Instead of confronting her about how much it hurt me, he said nothing.

Things like that happened all the time with him. Looking the other way when someone is rude at a restaurant. Saying nothing if he sees a neighbor take a package off someone's doorstep. Anything that could result in any kind of conflict he walked away from. I always chalked it up to him being sensitive or not liking confrontation. But now I wonder if he actually just doesn't care that much about anyone except himself.

How did I not see all these red flags before? Was I really that blind? Or was I too afraid to rock the boat—too afraid to lose the one relationship that I've ever had to see things how they really were?

"His mom never really liked me," I blurt out. "She included me in holidays and family vacations and stuff. But I always felt this vibe around her. Like I wasn't good enough for her precious baby boy."

"So he's a mama's boy. Makes perfect sense."

"She set him up on a date before he'd even broken up with me."

Lauren pulls back but stays silent.

No words.

Still quiet.

I take a chance and open my eyes to see a look of anger mixed with disbelief on her face. Her nostrils flare just slightly and her jaw is clenched as she shakes her head.

"That is some bullshit, Ellery. You don't deserve to be treated that way. What a piece of shit."

"Kevin or his mom?" I ask with a small laugh.

"Both. With a mom like that and him being such a fucking pushover, I guarantee the break-up had nothing to do with you. Hell, I'm not sure the last few years of your relationship did either. Sounds like it was all about him."

"I don't know if that makes me feel better or worse."

"That's part of the charm of relationships." Her sarcasm is thick. "You can't have the good without the bad. Next time I just hope you see the bad a little quicker. You deserve so much better than that."

Lauren puts down the mascara and claps her hands together, her expression drastically changing to one of excitement. "And we are about to find you so much better. Are you ready to look at yourself in the mirror?"

I hold my breath, anticipating some clown to stare back at me in the reflection. "No, not really."

"Too bad." She forces my chair around so I can see myself and I gasp.

I look like the girl in the picture on her phone. The one who was effortlessly glamorous and fashionable. That's me. Glamourous. And fashionable.

"How did you do that?" I breathe, leaning in closer to get a better look.

"It's the magic of makeup. It's really not that hard to do. But you see how it makes your hair almost like an accessory to your new look?"

I turn my head this way and that, stunned by the beautiful woman looking back at me. She looks confident and self-assured. She's the kind of woman people stare at on the street, not because they want to be with her but because they want to *be* her.

I want to be her.

I *am* her!

"I can't believe it, Lauren. I never knew I could look like this."

"You like it?"

"I love it. Thank you!"

I can't stop myself from turning and launching into her arms and giving her a hug. I feel like she's given me a gift. The gift of helping me find myself and who I want to be. I'm not there yet, but this is a better start than I could have imagined for myself.

Turning back to the mirror, I fluff my hair and press my lips together again.

Lauren, on the other hand, begins cleaning everything up. "Does this mean we're going out tonight?"

"By out, do you mean the bar?"

"Of course!" she says with a giggle. "I drink free there."

"You drink a lot there."

"Nah. I'm a social drinker. And I'm social with my friends. You guys don't see the massive amounts of lemon water and protein shakes Heath shoves in me during our everyday lives."

"I didn't know him that well in college but it seems like he's a great guy."

"He is." Her expression turns all dreamy and I try not to laugh. Lauren is always tough as nails so to see her melt into a puddle just at the thought of her boyfriend is really cute. Pulling herself back together quickly, she can't help but poke fun at me, too. "He's not the only great guy, you know."

Even through all the make-up, I see myself blush again. Lauren sees it too.

"You like him, don't you?" This is not a question. This is her trying to force me to admit what I'm trying to hold back. Of course, I cave.

"I really do," I breathe out, my shoulders dropping now that I've finally unloaded that burden. "But it was just a night of sex and I keep trying to remind myself of that. It didn't mean anything to either of us, even if he is sensitive and kind and smart—"

"And sexy as all hell."

"That too." I drop back down on the chair and move to prop my fist on my cheek but Lauren swats my hand away.

"Don't mess up your makeup."

"Sorry." Instead, I clasp my hands together. "Some woman is going to be super lucky to have Liam someday."

Lauren's brows furrow, looking at me like I've lost my mind. "Why can't that woman be you?"

"Because I'm me."

"You're looking at me like I should be agreeing with you right now but I don't. Kevin's mom messed with your brain more than you realize."

My phone alerts me of a message and I roll the chair to my purse. I'm sure I look like an idiot as I try to dig my heels into the tile to scooch across the floor.

"Do you see the choice I just made to get to my purse the hard way? I am not built to be the kind of woman Liam would be interested in for more than one night. I think I'm a little too immature." Finally reaching my purse, I blow out a breath from the exertion. "That was so much harder than I thought it would be."

Lauren snorts a laugh. "No doubt. But I don't think it

would be a deal-breaker for someone like Liam. For god's sake, twice, *twice* he's the one that approached you at the bar. Not the other way around."

I ignore her, and grab my phone, not wanting to get my hopes up. I'm not in any emotional position to wish for more. I went into that night knowing it wasn't the beginning of a relationship. If I allow myself to even consider that Liam likes me for more than what that one night was for, I'm sure to have my heart broken again.

As I slide open my phone, though, it would appear the universe does not agree.

"What?" Lauren asks. "Why do you look surprised all of a sudden?"

I laugh lightly at the irony I never saw coming.

Liam: Been thinking about you and would like to take you out on a real date. One that starts with great food and great company and ends with a chaste kiss at your doorstep so there's no question of how much I like you. Would you be interested in going on a date with me? If you're free, of course.

"Wait…" Lauren says because nothing gets by her. "Is that Liam?"

"Yep. And yes, you told me so."

She laughs loudly at this turn of events. "Did he ask you out? You're going to say yes, right? You're already made up and ready to go."

"But didn't you want to go out?"

She waves me off. "We can go out any night. I'll still be around and Heath leaves for training camp soon anyway so I'll be bored."

I bite my lip, unsure of what to do. On the one hand, I like Liam. More than I probably should admit to myself, but this text is making me think all kinds of things I probably shouldn't.

Still, I've missed out on building relationships with women for so many years by putting a man first and look where it got me. I don't want to do that again.

Lauren puts her hand on my arm, like she knows my internal struggle. "Take a chance on Liam. He's not Kevin. He's the exact opposite. He might be exactly what you need. And then," she adds with excitement in her eyes. "Come over tomorrow so we can hang by the pool and talk all about it."

I smile, grateful that she seems to understand my hesitation. I've missed her. I'm so glad she's back in my life.

Decision made, I click to reply.

Me: Pick me up at 8.

TEN

Liam

I chuckle when I knock on her front door, that Fourth of July wreath giving me way too much amusement. I don't know why it tickles me that it's still there. Maybe because it has me wondering if she's one of those people who decorate for the whole month. I hope I'm around long enough to find out. In my imagination, the Christmas holiday season is extra festive on this door.

I like Ellery. A lot. Not just because of what she can do in the bedroom, and holy shit can she do more than she even knew. I was expecting her lack of experience to make her more reserved but instead, she wanted to try everything. To do everything. I haven't been with a woman like that in, maybe ever.

But I like her for more than just the great sex. I like her dry sense of humor. I like that she's number smart. I like that she always shocks me with her determination to experience as much of life as she can. It seems so at odds with her reserved demeanor.

As she opens the door, I realize I like the way she looks

too because Holy. Shit.

"You look… wow," I breathe practically rendered speechless.

Her face flushes slightly, just like it does when she orgasms. Now is not the time to think about that, though. I'm here to take her on a proper date, not push her back into her apartment and ravage her. Although it is tempting…

"Lauren gave me a makeover today. You like it?"

"Yeah. I mean, I like you without it but you look so, so…"

"Hollywood glam?"

"That's it."

It's the exact right phrase, too. Her lips are bright red and her eyes pop somehow. Maybe it's the extra eyeliner she has or her lashes. I'm not sure, but the dark blue has just come alive. Her lavender-colored hair is sleek and smooth, one side pinned back. I know her clothes are on point, too, but I can't get past those pouty lips long enough to look harder at what she's wearing. She reminds me of a pin-up girl.

"Thank you. I honestly thought I was going to look like a clown when Lauren was done, but she's pretty talented with makeup brushes." Grabbing her purse from a small table, Ellery pulls the door closed behind her. "Are you ready to go?"

Taking her hand in mine, I intertwine our fingers, her tiny little fingers engulfed by my big paw. She smiles shyly but doesn't seem to mind. Slowly, we make our way to my truck.

"Where would you like to go for our first official date?" I know it may be early to allude to having more dates in the future but I've never met anyone like this woman. I don't want her second-guessing my intentions.

"I hadn't thought about it. I just assumed you'd decide."

"I almost did but then I realized I'd like to take you someplace you enjoy."

Ellery thinks and then settles for the cop-out. "What do you like?"

I give her a pointed look. "I didn't ask where I'd like to go. I'm trying to make you happy. What do you like? What is your favorite restaurant or bar? Favorite food on a night out."

"I…" She blinks a few times, truly and completely stumped. "I don't know."

"Really? Or is this one of those things women say because they want French fries, tacos, and cheesecake and you can't get all that at the same place?"

Ellery bites her plump red lip, which she seems to do a lot when she's nervous. I hope I have a chance to bite it later. "I never thought about what I like before. Kevin used to just know where he wanted to go and I guess it's in my nature to care about what others think. I'm so sorry," she backpedals quickly her face pinkening again. "I can't believe I brought up my ex-boyfriend while I'm on a date with you. That was so rude. I'm really not missing him, I swear."

"Ellery," I say with my most reassuring voice knowing she's kicking herself internally. "It doesn't bother me if you bring him up. You were with him for a long time and it's still new to be without him. He's still going to cross your mind for a while. Just because I'm taking you out, doesn't mean I want you to censor your thoughts." I open the truck door and guide her in the seat before asking her the question I know is going to be hard for her to answer. "But let me ask you something, do you really have no preference about where we eat? Or did that idiot never ask your opinion, so you've forgotten what you like?"

She blinks rapidly for a few seconds. Like I thought, I've stumped her. "I've always wanted to go to a hibachi grill," she finally blurts out in a rush.

I smile in response, glad to see she's starting to feel confident enough to tell me what she wants, and a little excited to get some ideas for my own recipes. "Then Hibachi it is. Watch your legs."

I shut her in and make my way around the front of the cab, happy to have her sharing her opinions. Where to eat may be a small one, but I'm interested to know what she thinks about a lot of things, so I call this a win.

The drive to the place I know is about fifteen minutes. Long enough to make small talk about her job and some big promotion she seems really excited about. We talk about my love of cooking and the homemade Alfredo sauce I'm trying to perfect. She asks about my practice schedule during the off-season which I have no problem answering. But I deflect any questions related to my surgery. It'll just put me in a bad mood and I don't want that for our first official date. I don't want it for any date, actually. But this one, in particular, seems special. Not just for me, but for her, and I want her to have good memories of it to fall back on when I'm out of commission for a couple of months.

The restaurant parking lot is pretty full, but I finally find a space and pull in.

"Should we have gotten a reservation?" Ellery asks as she looks around.

"For two of us, I don't think it'll take too long. They'll probably slide us in at a table with a family to fill in the last couple of spots anyway."

Her eyes widen in surprise. "We won't sit alone? We'll

be with other people?"

"Oh yeah. It's a lot of fun. You ready to make some new dinner friends?"

She nods excitedly and I'm pleased at how much fun she's already having and we're not even inside yet.

Pulling the door open, Ellery's eyes close and she takes a full breath in, enjoying the wonderful smell of Japanese food. When her eyes open again, she takes in the room, delight dancing in her eyes.

It's a fairly stereotypical restaurant. Close to a dozen tables set for eight with a grill built into each one, are scattered around an open room that boasts lots of woodwork and decorative art pieces.

I hold up two fingers when the hostess asks how many are in our party and am pretty excited when she immediately seats us along with a family of five.

"Wow, you weren't kidding we wouldn't have to wait for long," Ellery remarks as we sit.

"That was sheer luck. So, what do you think of your first hibachi grill experience so far?"

She looks around, nodding in greeting at the other adults at our table, which I assume are the parents of the kids also sitting with us.

"I'm really excited to see things catch on fire."

I bark out a laugh at her candor. "Yeah, that is pretty exciting. Hand me your phone."

Her brow furrows slightly. "What?"

I hold my hand out. "Your phone. I assume you're going to want some pictures of your reaction the first time the flames jump."

"Uh, no. I think it's best if there is no record of how dumb I look when I squeal or whatever."

I shrug knowing I have a phone too and I'll be documenting this experience even if she doesn't know it.

Just then our teppanyaki chef arrives and the show begins.

Ellery orders a shrimp dinner and I go with the chicken. My stomach grumbles and I'm looking forward to dinner, but not before the magic happens.

Our chef flips and spears and lights things on fire. I get several candid shots of Ellery and her reactions. We also laugh when one of the kids at our table begins crying, afraid her food is "going to be burnt up". We have a great time and our chef puts on an amazing show.

When we're finally tucked into our dinners, things get quieter and open up the opportunity for more conversation.

"Was your first time here everything you hoped it would be?"

I assume it is. The smile hasn't left her face since we got here, but I want to hear it straight from her.

"More. That thing he did when the flame got so big—I thought he was going to burn the place down!"

"I still can't believe you've never come to a place like this before."

She swallows some rice before responding. "Kevin is an inspector for the health department so he doesn't make a lot of money. A place like this was out of his budget."

I highly doubt that, but if it's what Ellery wants to believe, there's no harm in it. It just means I lose a little more respect for the guy. I can't help but wonder if he's one of those guys who has a health department badge he wears around so he can pretend he has some kind of authority over people.

Seriously, the more I know about him, the less I like him.

"Good food is never out of my budget," I joke, trying

to lighten up my own feelings on the matter.

"I'm with you there. This is amazing. And I'm surprised how comfortable it is sitting with strangers."

One of the kids across from us flips a pea at her brother with a spoon, nailing him in the forehead. We both laugh at their antics.

"You ever want kids?" I ask. "Not now, I mean. But in the future."

She thinks for a second as she chews and swallows. "I think so."

"You don't sound very sure."

"I've always assumed I'd have them, just never put much thought into when. I was an only child and my parents had me when they were older so I guess it seems like I've got a lot of time. What about you? Do you have brothers and sisters?"

"Two sisters actually. Both younger so I feel like I've already raised some kids."

Ellery giggles. "I'm sure your mother would disagree with you about that."

"Oh, I know she would. She has no understanding of the sense of responsibility big brothers feel."

"I like that you love them so much. Do they live close?"

"Nah. They're in Vancouver."

Her fork pauses mid-air. "You're Canadian?"

Her reaction makes me smile. People around here are always surprised to find out I'm technically a foreigner. "Yeah. Is that a problem?"

"If you tell me that you're friends with Justin Bieber, I may have to reconsider this relationship."

"Ha. Ha. And you tell Matthew McConoughey I said hi next time you see him."

Ellery pushes her now empty bowl away with a smile.

"Seriously, though. That must have been a huge change, just in climate. Canada to Central Texas?"

"I admit, I spent more time on the ice than necessary just to cool off when I first got here. I think my body was in shock."

"So, you've been playing hockey your whole life then?"

"Pretty much." My stomach clenches at the reminder that it could all be going up in smoke if this surgery doesn't go as planned. And unlike our dinner, there's no one to fix my career if it does.

Based on the look in her eyes, she knows we're veering into difficult territory.

"When is your surgery?" she asks quietly.

Having lost my appetite, I push my bowl away, too, and quickly wave off a server who offers us dessert.

"Wednesday."

"You nervous?"

"Not about the surgery."

"You're nervous about your ability to play again."

I glance up at her seeing nothing but compassion in her eyes. It isn't pity. It's like a genuine understanding of what I'm going through.

"How did you know?"

"I don't remember if I told you I was a competitive gymnast all the way through college." I nod, vaguely remembering something about it from a couple of weeks ago. "Injuries weren't uncommon and by college, you're at the tail end of your career. It was so much harder to make a comeback after surgery at twenty-one than it was at fifteen. I don't know exactly how old you are, but I assume you aren't twenty-one anymore and you get kind of stiff whenever the surgery comes up in conversation. Obviously, I'm jumping to conclusions, but am I close?"

I'm impressed with her ability to deduce why this is hard for me. And admittedly, it's a tiny bit nice knowing she understands how I feel. She's not a gymnast anymore and she's found a place for herself. It's not encouraging per se, but I suppose it takes a bit of the edge off.

"I'm thirty-one. Most guys are already retired by this age. I honestly don't know if I'll have a job six months from now because of all this."

Ellery puts her hand on mine and I immediately flip it over so our fingers clasp together.

"I can imagine how scary that is."

"What am I going to do if I can't come back from this?"

I'm shocked by my own candor. It was one thing to share this question with my coach. I'm not the first one he's pushed into retirement. He's seen the outcome before and has networks he can reach out to if I need them. But it isn't Ellery's job to push me out of my comfort zone and help me find who I am outside of the sport I love. Yet here she is, looking at me with such understanding it makes it easy for me to open up. Almost too easy.

"You find something new that you love almost as much as hockey."

"That's accounting for you?"

"Oddly, yes. I like the stability of numbers. That there's always a right and wrong answer. There's no grey area to sort through. For me, the repetition is almost calming."

I want to ask her more. Like how she discovered her love of numbers and when she knew it was the career path she wanted to take. But this conversation has started to take a depressing turn that I don't like.

Clearing my throat, I gesture for the bill. "Well, maybe I'll find something I like just as much at some point."

Seeming to recognize that I want to move on, Ellery shifts in her seat, no longer leaning in as close as she was. I'm grateful to move on to lighter topics, but not thrilled about her distance.

"Do you already have a ride home from the hospital and someone staying with you?" she asks with a nonchalance I appreciate.

"Tucker… you know Tucker Hayes?"

"I don't think so."

"He's the guy who makes me go to Trivia Night at the bar and wear an ugly green shirt."

"Ah," she says with a smile. "And he's terrible at pool."

I smile at the memory of him getting whooped by Dwayne the first night she and I met. "That's him. He's a good friend and is going to get me home."

"But what about after?"

"I've hired an at-home nurse to help me for a few days."

By the look on her face, she's not pleased with my answer. "There's no one else who can stay with you? No one from your family can come?"

"From Canada? Nah. They all have their own lives."

She gives me a look of understanding. "You didn't tell them about it did you?"

I look away, embarrassed to have been caught. It seemed like the best idea before, but now that she's called me out, it feels a little different.

Tossing my credit card on the bill without looking at the total, I try to deflect. "There's no reason to worry them unless I have to. I love my mom but she would freak out more than necessary."

Ellery assesses me, searching for a lie I'm sure, but there is none. It's not the whole truth—I just didn't want to tell them. But I'm not wrong about my mom either.

Satisfied with my explanation, she nods once. "Can I at least come over and help you in the evenings after work? Cook you real food instead of letting you subsist on take-out until you can meal prep again? You are an athlete after all. Three months of junk food won't help you get back on the ice."

"You don't have to cook, but I won't turn down the attention of a beautiful woman."

"It's probably better if I don't cook," she admits. "Unlike one of us, it's not my forte. But I can order a mean grilled chicken salad from this great deli by my house."

"Sounds perfect."

We head to the car and drive around for a little bit, with nothing to do. I'd love to keep her out longer, but with surgery coming up, I'm putting in extra work at the arena while I can. Ellery doesn't seem to mind.

As I drop her at her apartment and walk her to her doorstep, I leave her with a not-so-chaste kiss, just like I promised.

ELEVEN

Ellery

I t's the second time I've been to Lauren's house in two days. Not that I'm complaining. The house itself is incredible with huge vaulted ceilings and an airy open floor plan. It's exactly what I would expect a professional football player to live in. Although I do wonder if it was Heath or Lauren who chose this place.

Even more exciting to me, though, is the company. When Liam and I made plans for our date last night, Lauren demanded I come over for lunch so I could tell her all about it. I jumped at the chance because it feels so good to have a female friend that cares about my date.

I only wait a few seconds after ringing the bell for the huge door to fly open. Only it's not Lauren answering.

"Ellery! You made it!" Kiersten reaches in for a hug and then pulls me into the house. "Lauren is making some sangria to go with the charcuterie board."

I follow Kiersten into the kitchen where Lauren is stirring a purplish drink full of various fruit in a glass pitcher.

"Hey! You're here!" she greets me with a smile and

gestures to her left. "Do you know Kiersten's sister Nicole?"

The beautiful blonde bartender waves from the island stool she's sitting on.

"I've seen you at the bar but we haven't been introduced. I'm Ellery."

"Nice to meet you, Ellery. Thanks for letting me crash your girls' day. I don't get time to do it very often."

"I actually didn't know it was going to be girls' day. Not the I'm complaining," I tack on quickly not wanting to offend. "I don't get to hang out with women very often either."

"I wasn't sure if you'd be up for coming over after your big date last night." Lauren waggles her eyebrows and I can't help but wonder if she's already started drinking the sangria.

"We weren't out late. Liam wanted to practice early this morning so we just had dinner and then called it a night."

Lauren wrinkles her nose. "So, no hot sex then."

I can feel my face flame. "No. But dinner was hot. He took me to a hibachi grill."

Kiersten grabs an olive off the wooden board and pops it in her mouth. "Oooh! I love those places. Nic, isn't your anniversary coming up? You should get Kade to take you. You'd love it."

I'm not positive who Kade is but I vaguely remember hearing something about him working at the bar, too. Now it makes sense as to why no one was hitting on her while she was working the other day, though. She's already taken.

"Forget me," Nicole says. "Watching someone use heavy knives to slaughter our dinner before setting it on fire? That sounds right up my boyfriend's alley."

All my new friends continue chatting about different restaurants in the area and picking various cheese and meats off the board to snack on. It's very relaxed and I find myself easing into the conversations with no problem whatsoever.

"What's Kade doing today anyway?" Lauren asks Nicole as she herds us out to the large covered back patio that is clearly used for entertaining on a regular basis. My eyes take in the backyard and how immaculate it all is. From the huge fenced-in pool to the fully loaded outdoor kitchen, it's like a little oasis.

"He's gaming for a little bit before he goes into work," Nicole says as she makes herself comfortable on a wicker swing that looks like she's sitting inside an Easter egg.

"Paul's working, too?" Lauren asks, plopping down next to Kiersten who is carefully laying the charcuterie board on the table. Lauren isn't quite as gentle with the pitcher when she puts it down in front of her.

Kiersten takes a sip of her drink before answering. "Can you believe it? I can't remember the last time Lauren and I had the same night off to just hang out. Not that we can hang out for long. Mom duty and all that."

"We'll just move the party to your place so we can hang out with Carson," Lauren suggests. "I'm sure he won't mind us coming over."

Kiersten snorts a laugh. "You mean so he can swindle you out of any change you have in your purse?"

Lauren holds up her hand. "Listen, blame Heath. All I did was teach Carson how to play Kings in a Corner because I read somewhere it would help him with his math skills. His favorite uncle is the one who turned it into a gambling game." Ignoring Kiersten's eye roll, Lauren continues. "Actually, I have a better idea. Why doesn't Paul just drop Carson here? That way we don't have to drive anywhere and Heath can become victim to the little gambling addict he created instead of him bleeding me dry."

"Where is Heath anyway?" I ask, realizing I haven't seen him in his own house at all the last two days.

"At the gym," Lauren and Kiersten say simultaneously and then start laughing.

It's so strange seeing how in sync this group of friends is. I've known Kiersten and Lauren for years and yet I don't seem to know them at all. At least not with the same kind of closeness they seem to have with each other. Once again, I'm hit with how much I missed by keeping my focus on Kevin and Kevin alone. I never want to do that again.

"Which is probably the same place Liam is, right?" Kiersten asks as I settle myself deeper onto the most comfortable lounge chair I've ever sat on.

"Perks of dating an athlete," Lauren adds. "They've got rock-hard bodies for a reason. If they're not at home, they're somewhere sculpting those abs."

Ignoring Lauren's waggling eyebrows, Kiersten gets back to the one topic I'm nervous to discuss but really need some female perspective on. "How is it going with Liam, anyway? Do you *like him* like him?"

I do. I really do. But being here makes me wonder if this is all too rushed. Like maybe I'm moving too quickly. Am I doing the same thing with Liam that I did with Kevin—putting the man so far in front of my priorities that I miss out on everything else?

"I really do, but, well…." I bite my lip as I consider how to phrase my question. "Do you think it's too much too fast?"

"Because you just broke up with Kevin?" Lauren asks.

I shrug. "Well, yeah. Maybe? I'm starting to think I did my relationship with Kevin wrong."

"How so?" Nicole asks

"Like... I know you're supposed to put your partner first and all that. But, I think maybe I did that to the extreme and ended up putting myself... last."

All three of them nod and murmur things like "been there" and "it's so easy to do." Their confirmation that maybe I'm not the only one who's gotten myself in a precarious situation makes me feel a little less embarrassed about the whole thing.

"I can't speak for Kevin," Kiersten says, "Because I don't know him except for in passing a couple of times when we would go dancing way back when. But I think if you like Liam, go for it."

Lauren pops a cheese cube in her mouth and wipes her hands together. "I agree. I've known both of these guys and trust me, Liam is nothing like Kevin. For starters, he's less of a follower."

Kiersten nods vigorously. "This is true. He's not as..." she bobbles her head for a second before deciding on her words. "...flirtatious as say, Tucker Hayes."

Nicole giggles and covers her mouth and I suspect there's a story there but I don't ask, too curious about Kiersten's assessment.

"But he's a great guy. Doesn't really date much that I've seen."

"Really?" This information is such a surprise. I've just assumed Liam dated around and that's what we're doing. Or at least what he's doing. I'm enjoying myself maybe a little too much. "He doesn't date?"

Kiersten pulls her legs up, folding them underneath

her. "I'm not sure he's ever been opposed to dating. He just has never been the type to pick up a woman in a bar. He must think you're really special to break his normal pattern."

Her kind words make me feel fluttery inside. It's been a long time since another woman has given me a compliment like that. I forgot how nice they feel.

"He's no dummy," Lauren adds. "If he hadn't seen you first, someone else would have. Ellery, you're a catch. You're smart, beautiful, successful. Kevin is… nice?"

"You don't sound convinced," I say with a laugh.

"I'm not. In his case, nice is a cover for being a pushover." I can't say I disagree with Lauren there. "But Kevin's also not that impressive. He's kind of meh. You were always way above his pay grade."

"So, what you're saying is, I should stop overthinking whatever is happening with Liam and go for it."

One of her shoulders shrugs. "Listen, the worst thing that could happen is you have a little fun, have some great sex, and then you go your separate ways with more knowledge about how good a relationship can be. But the best that could happen?" Lauren's sigh has a dreamy quality to it. "The best could completely change your life."

I think that might be part of what I'm afraid of.

TWELVE

Liam

There is an unwritten rule that if you really like someone, you're supposed to wait three days after going on a date to text them and ask them out again.

I've never been good at following the rules.

My impatience didn't surprise me nearly as much as Ellery agreeing to let me make her a low-key dinner at my place tonight. Maybe it's because we had a great time at the hibachi grill last night. Maybe it's because she doesn't feel like cooking. Or maybe it's because I reminded her that my surgery is in a couple of days and I have no idea how long it'll be until I can take her out again.

It was a bit of a cheap shot to use my injury to my advantage like that, but I like Ellery and I really wanted to see her again.

Doing a quick once over to make sure no dirty socks are sticking out from under the couch or something, I nod, satisfied that my bachelor pad looks like a responsible man lives here at least.

My two-year-old grey cat, Patches, jumps up on the

back of the couch and runs his face up against me, ensuring a few pets from me. But only until the doorbell rings.

"Sorry buddy." He gives me the cat equivalent of the evil eye as I leave him to greet my guest. "Important people are waiting."

Swinging the door open, I take in Ellery's appearance. Her hair is up in a messy bun thing and her makeup is much lighter than last night. She looks sun-kissed and relaxed. I like this look on her.

Her nose crinkles just slightly. "I hope you don't mind. I came straight from Lauren's house. We were just hanging out so I didn't bother going home to change."

"No, no. Please come in." I wave her in and shut the door behind her. "Like I said, low-key." I gesture down to my athletic shorts and bare feet. "I just feel bad I pulled you away from your friends. We could have done this a different day."

She looks around my place while we chat. I wonder what she sees. A space well-maintained by a meticulous guy? A bachelor pad with more warmth than most?

"It's fine. Perfect, actually. Once Kiersten's son showed up and brought out a deck of cards, I knew it was time for me to leave." She laughs to herself. I don't understand whatever the joke is, but I don't need to. She's happy and she's here. That's all I need.

Just then, Patches begins rubbing up against her leg.

"Oh! Who's this?" Ellery exclaims and reaches down to pick up my cat. He begins purring immediately.

"That little attention hound is Patches."

"What? Why would you call him such a thing?" she coos in his face. "He's just a sweety pie, aren't you?"

If I'm not mistaken, the cat gives me a smug look, like getting all my date's attention is payback for my lack of chin scratches a few minutes ago. Bastard.

"Do you have any pets?"

"No." She continues scratching his head, cradling him like a baby. "I almost got a kitten once but Kevin was allergic," she says sheepishly.

"Well, you're in luck. No allergies here."

She follows me as I turn back to the kitchen, still holding Patches.

"It smells good in here. What are you making?"

The timer begins the thirty second count down so I grab my oven gloves to remove the food from my double oven.

"I'm trying a new recipe. There's lemon chicken on the bottom and I'm pulling out some roasted veggies now. I'll start the couscous in a minute."

"That sounds amazing." Ellery puts Patches on the floor and leans up against the kitchen island. "Have you always loved to cook?"

I drop the tray on the stovetop and begin grinding salt and pepper onto the veggies. A twinge of pain from the twisting runs through my shoulder but I put it out of my brain quickly. I refuse to let it ruin my mood while she's here.

"Not really," I say with a chuckle. "Cooking was just a necessity while growing up. Divorced parents, mom working late, three kids that needed to be fed. Same story as just about everyone."

"You're self-taught, then?"

"Yep. The older I got and the more I got into hockey, the less I could rely on frozen pizzas and fish sticks. I started sending grocery lists to my parents when I would find recipes. My mom indulged me and always got what I needed."

"Not your dad?"

"Seemed kind of pointless, and in his defense, he was right. We were only there every other weekend and eating out was something we liked to do. It was fine. I got a lot of recipe ideas from those places. Anyway, after a while cooking became sort of a comfort. Like a creative outlet or something. I like messing with recipes and seeing what I can do with them now."

"Well, it smells great."

I smile at her and open the second oven, pulling out the tray. Cutting into the chicken, I realize it needs just a few more minutes. Perfect. That's how long I need for the couscous to fluff just right.

"So, tell me, Ellery, when you aren't working, what do you like to do to unwind?"

She opens her mouth to speak but closes it quickly, a confused look on her face. I don't say anything, just let her think on her answer until she's finally ready.

"I don't really know. I've just realized in the last couple of weeks that I've not really made any effort to try things outside of work and one failed relationship. Before that, it was all gymnastics all the time. I guess you could say I'm on a journey to figure out what my interests are."

Her answer doesn't totally shock me. Although her honesty is a bit of a surprise. Just last night she had a hard time giving her opinion on a restaurant but here she is recognizing she's got a lot of exploring to do.

"Think cooking might be one of them?"

Ellery holds her hand up. "I can honestly say there is not one part of me that is remotely interested in helping you right now. Watching you cook is probably more my speed."

I chuckle at her candor. "Well at least you eliminated one potential hobby before you sunk a bunch of money into small appliances."

We continue to chat about our lives, just getting to know each other. For someone who doesn't know what her interests are, she's really interesting herself. Her thoughts on new tax laws are surprisingly engaging considering I have a financial advisor to worry about all that shit.

But it isn't until we're sitting down to eat that I realize how much I could get used to this. Having her here, just talking about nothing special.

Tucking her legs under her, I present Ellery with lemon chicken and roasted spring veggies on a bed of freshly made couscous. Her eyes light up and she licks her lips, ready to dig in.

Taking her first bite, Ellery moans and I feel it all the way into my groin.

"Oh wow, this is so good." She takes a second bite, closing her eyes to savor as she chews.

I, on the other hand, have lost my ability to eat, too focused on the look on her face.

Ellery's eyes open and she goes for another bite, but stops when she makes eye contact with me.

Her eyes dart around quickly. "What?"

"I can't eat when you moan like that."

A blush immediately creeps up her face, but then she surprises me once again. Carefully placing her fork down, Ellery wipes her mouth with her napkin, pushes away from the table, and walks toward me. I watch, barely breathing, waiting to see what she does next. I'm not disappointed when she straddles me and sits on my lap, wrapping her arms around my neck.

Our lips fuse together and I'm lost in this woman. This tiny, petite thing can disarm me with one look on her face, one moan, one kiss, one impromptu climb onto my lap.

As our tongues tangle, my hips begin to rock, getting nowhere and doing nothing to ease the tension in my groin.

Grabbing her by the thighs, I walk over to the kitchen island and sit her on top, giving myself the ability to grind into her.

Ellery gasps at the feel. "Are we about to have kitchen sex?" Her eyes light up as she says it.

"Only if you want to."

"Oh, I want to."

That's all I need to hear and apparently all she needs to say. We're suddenly ripping at each other's clothes, desperate to get each other naked.

"I really enjoyed our date last night," Ellery breathes. "But I've been hoping to get back to the sex."

I smile at her words. "Leaving you with just a peck was the hardest thing I've ever done. I had to whack in the shower last night. Twice."

Ellery pulls back to look at me, lips swollen from my kisses. "That is the sexiest thing I've ever heard."

"As sexy as me saying I'm about to fuck you on this counter?"

"No, yeah, *that* was the sexiest thing I've ever heard."

We continue pulling at each other's clothing until we're finally both naked and ready. My hands run all over her smooth skin, pulling her body closer to the edge of the counter.

"Condom," she breathes.

Reaching behind her, I pull open a drawer, riffle around for a second before producing the prize. Ellery starts laughing.

"Why do you have a condom in your kitchen?"

I shrug. "It's a junk drawer. No idea how the condom got there, but I happened to see it this morning."

She laughs again but abruptly stops to watch me slide the condom over my length. Biting her lip, Ellery's eyes look back and forth from my cock to my eyes and back to my cock again. As soon as I'm sheathed, she wraps her legs around me and pulls me toward her, not wanting to waste any time.

"Are you ready?" I murmur against her lips.

"Ready. Don't go slow."

That's all the encouragement I need.

We both groan as I plunge inside her. I pause so she can adjust to me and to give myself a second to control the orgasm that already wants to take over. Once I'm satisfied we're both good to go, the frenzy begins.

I thrust hard and fast, spurred on by Ellery's moans and words of approval.

"Lay back, baby."

She does as I ask, leaning on her elbows, eyes glued to the place where we connect. Watching her watch us makes me almost blow. Instead, I bend her knees, placing her feet on the counter so I can get deeper. In mere seconds, Ellery's head falls back and her arms give out as the orgasm rips through her body.

I let go and join her, never taking my eyes off the look on her face as she comes. My orgasm slams into me making me nearly collapse on top of her from the sheer force.

As we come down from our high, both of us breathing heavily, I'm hit with the thought that this is it for me. Ellery is it for me. I don't want anyone else. Ever.

It's a heavy thought and yet, not one that scares me at all. In fact, it feels exactly right. I'll just have to wait until she's as ready as I am.

As she runs her hands down my back, I kiss Ellery's neck and shoulder and jaw. Small pecks of appreciation and gentle emotion.

"That was amazing," she says with a sigh. "Can't wait to find out what's for dessert."

I bark out a laugh because I know what I'm planning to eat.

And I do. Right on that same counter again.

THIRTEEN
Ellery

It's been two days since my first experience at a hibachi grill. It's been one day since kitchen sex. It's been non-stop texting with Liam the whole time.

We've had in-depth conversations about heavy subjects, and light conversations about day-to-day stuff. Nothing seems off-limits and my cheeks hurt from smiling so much.

I hate it.

Mostly I hate that I really like it. I like *him*. But I don't want to get caught up in a man and lose myself again. I'm finally discovering things about myself I didn't know before. Who knew I wasn't a fan of reality television but enjoy documentaries about the history of ghost towns? Or that I enjoy looking through fashion magazines? And that I might want a second piercing in my ear sometime in the future? I didn't know any of that until the last couple of weeks when I've had total control over my apartment.

I can't stop thinking about what Liam meant when he asked if I really didn't know where I like to eat or if Kevin just never bothered asking for my opinion. I fear Liam nailed a lot of things about me with that one question.

For instance, am I truly a nurturing person, or do I hide from disappointment by always putting others first? Am I just a run-of-the-mill people pleaser or is it in my nature to worry about other people's opinions? Have I been too scared to try new things and what would I try now if I could?

An alert pops up indicating I have a new email. Quickly I flip screens. I've been crunching payroll numbers for one of our clients for several hours. My brain is losing focus.

It's from Mrs. Welch titled, "Join me in giving congratulations to Peter Madden."

Congratulations? What in the world are we congratulating him for?

Scanning the email, my jaw drops with disbelief.

As you know, we have been in the market for a new senior accountant. We are pleased to announce, after much discussion, Peter Madden has accepted our offer to fill that role."

My breathing picks up, my blood boiling. I have been here longer than Peter Madden. I have more experience, a higher customer appreciation rate, a lower mistake percentage. I work any overtime Mrs. Welch asks of me without complaint and wear suits from the same store she purchases from.

That job was supposed to be mine. She told me as much over Easter brunch. But that was before Kevin and I broke up. Before she set him up on a blind date with another woman.

The realization literally knocks me backward in my

chair.

The only reason she gave me this job, the only reason she considered me for the senior accountant position is because of him. Now that he's moved on, per her request, that's all over.

All those years of busting my tail, thinking I'm getting ahead because I'm good at my job and have a solid work ethic for what? To get overlooked for *Peter Madden*? I didn't even get an interview. Is my current job in jeopardy, too?

My anger and disappointment are too high to worry about potential unemployment right now. I need to get out of here.

I push my chair back, then stop, Liam's words running through my head again.

"Do you really have no preference or have you forgotten what you like?"

He's right. I have forgotten. Things I've wanted to try, never even considered because they might be frowned upon. Places I've wanted to go, never to be seen because someone might want to go somewhere else. Conservative hair, conservative makeup, conservative clothes because the boss might give me a promotion.

Well, no more. As of this moment, I'm going to begin taking chances and living a little.

Quickly, I grab a pencil, because it's always best to make notes with something erasable, and begin jotting down a list.

Ellery's To-Do List
    1. Create a social media account

    2. Go to a BTS concert

3. Get a second piercing

4. Get a tattoo. Maybe.

I begin to jot down a fifth item when I remember I'm trying to seize the day, not plan for tomorrow. Instead, I pick up my cell, scroll for the number I'm looking for and make a call.

Five minutes later, I grab my purse and head out my door.

"I'm taking a long lunch," I say to Brittany, the front desk receptionist in passing.

"Okay?" I can hear the confusion in her voice as I walk toward the elevator. I've never taken a long lunch in the over five years I've worked here. "Is everything alright, Ellery?"

I turn and give her a tight-lipped smile, not wanting to give anything away. "Just peachy."

Thankfully, the door to the lift opens and I hurry inside, ready to get away from this place and work on myself for a little bit.

My drive is a little longer than normal with lunchtime traffic, but I have no desire to go back to work any time soon so I don't care. I'm a woman on a mission.

When I finally reach my destination, I strut in, determination on my face.

"Hi, can I help you?" a pleasant woman asks at the desk.

Suddenly I deflate just a little. What am I doing? Do I really want to take this step or am I reacting in anger to the betrayals I feel at the hands of my boss?

I'm about to cancel my appointment when my stylist Jayden appears out of nowhere.

"Ellery! You made it!" She greets me with a hug and

practically drags me back to her chair.

I haven't been here in a couple of months, and long before my hair coloring debacle at home.

"How have you been?" She asks as she drapes the cape around me. "And who did this color? It looks amazing on you!"

"Really?"

"Truly. I absolutely love it. Are we touching it up today?"

I take a deep breath, trying to tap back into the anger and courage I was feeling a few minutes ago.

"I want to do something a little different."

"Sure. Are we adding layers or maybe some streaks of something brighter?" She runs her fingers through my hair, giving my head a thorough exam.

"I want to cut it all off."

Jayden's fingers freeze. "What?"

"You heard me."

"That is a pretty drastic change. Are you sure?"

I nod, feeling my confidence return. "I've always wanted to try a pixie cut but I've been worried no one would like it. But I played around online the other day with one of those apps that let you try out different haircuts and I think it'll look good."

She circles the chair and me in it, assessing my face from different angles. "Your bone structure will really come alive with shorter hair. But you have to be absolutely sure. Once I make the first cut, there's no going back. It's not like we're just going to your shoulders and it's easy to grow back."

"I'm sure. Let's do it."

She moves behind me, picking up the scissors and a large chunk of my hair. Making eye contact in the mirror, she puts the scissors in position and pauses.

"Last chance."

I take a deep breath before pulling my shoulders back. "Do it."

The snip only takes a few seconds but the weight that feels lifted as my hair falls to the floor is tremendous. This is me taking control of my life. Trying new things and figuring out how I want to live. This is me saying "forget what anyone else thinks—it's my life and I'll do things how I want."

This is me, finally freeing myself from other people's expectations and working on being the best version of me that I can be. Whatever she looks like.

Once my hair is short, Jayden does a thorough wash and condition, spouting off information about how to take care of my new color. It's welcome advice considering the color was such an impulsive move on my part, I hadn't even thought about upkeep.

When I sit back in the chair though, she doesn't let me face the mirror. I've already seen the beginnings of me with super short hair, but knowing she wants to surprise me with the finished product eases the nerves I feel and makes me excited.

"With hair this short, you're going to need to come back every couple of weeks so we can trim the back," she instructs as clippers graze the back of my neck. It tickles and I have to force myself to sit still. "Also, next time, let's touch up your color so we can keep it looking fresh, okay?"

"Okay," I say rather than nod for fear I'll end up with a random shaved stripe on the back of my head.

"It's a lot to maintain, but this looks so amazing." A dollop of some sort of product goes on her hands and into my hair. She rubs her hands to and fro until she's finally satisfied that my hair is the exact right version of messy. Or sleek. I'm not sure yet since I haven't seen it.

When she stands back to observe the final product, she gasps. "Ohmygod Ellery. You are stunning."

I bite my lip as she spins my chair around and get my first glimpse of the new me.

I swear I stop breathing as I take in the beautiful woman in front of me. The very short, pixie cut has a bit of a purposeful mess to it. Somehow the length makes the color pop even more and my neck looks longer. Elegant. The woman in the mirror, she looks bold and confident, ready to take on the world. But there's one thing missing.

"Can you hand me my purse?"

She does and I take out my other new indulgence—the cherry red lip color Lauren swears pulls my new make-up look together. Freshening up the application that wore off earlier in the day, I take another look at myself.

Perfect.

"Ohmygod Ellery," Jayden breathes. "I knew this would look great on you but I had no idea."

"Me neither."

After a few more minutes of gazing at the beauty in the mirror, I check out and head back to my workday. I never did have lunch, but I can survive off the granola bars stashed in my desk drawer that I keep for unexpected late nights.

Making my way from the parking lot into the building, I notice the double takes I'm getting. There aren't many, just other people who work in this complex, but it still gives me a huge boost to my ego. I went for it, tried something new, and so far, I love it.

It isn't until I get on the elevator that I begin to question myself and the way I left. I stormed out after getting an email that hurt my feelings. I wasn't professional and didn't even consult the dress code before making a rash decision.

But then the doors close and I see my reflection.

I look professional and well put together. I look like a woman who can handle anything that is thrown her way. I look like a woman who can handle anything a *client* throws her way. My nerves calm as I remember that not only will I make an amazing first impression from here on out, I made great first impressions before. At minimum, I should have been interviewed for that senior accountant position. But I wasn't bold enough to be memorable. Now, as I look at the new me, I realize bold is my new motto. My new goal.

Armed with that realization, I sashay my way into the office and past Brittany who almost drops the phone receiver as I walk by, and Mrs. Welch who just happens to be standing at her desk.

"I'm back," I say and then add a quick nod in greeting to my boss as I saunter by.

Not surprising because of the complete look of shock on both their faces, they don't respond.

Finally, in the safety of my office, I shove my purse into my desk drawer and pull out my phone to shoot off a text to Lauren.

Me: Meet me at the bar tonight. I have something to show you.

Pleased with myself, I get back to work. These numbers won't crunch themselves and even if Mrs. Welch doesn't see my value, I do.

I won't let the client down no matter how mad I am about *Peter Madden*. I'm better than that. And I have no one to prove it to except myself.

FOURTEEN

Liam

"**W**ho am I supposed to scrimmage with when you're off the ice?"

Tucker Hayes, my teammate and probably closest friend continues to bitch about how hard my surgery is going to make his life. Not shocking. He's a great guy but a bit of a drama queen at times.

"You're not." I've known him long enough to not be offended by Tucker's uncanny ability to make any situation about himself. He'll vent for a while before realizing what he's doing and getting back on track. "You're supposed to go on vacation, maybe visit your family. All those things you can't do once pre-season starts."

He swallows his beer with a sigh and continues to stare at the bartender he's been crushing on for months. "You know that's not me. I'm a homebody."

"No, you're not. You're just still pining over a certain blonde who will never consider you more than just a friend."

Just then, Nicole's live-in boyfriend, Kade, walks by

and slaps her on the ass. She startles and then smiles lovingly at him and shakes her head.

"It's never going to happen," Tucker says wistfully before shaking it off and turning to me. "But you can't blame me for still having fantasies about her."

"I can and I do," I say, pointing my bottle at him. "It's been months since she turned you down. It's time to move on and let those love birds be."

"I know, I know. It would just be easier if we could meet some new people somewhere."

"You mean like… on vacation?"

He scowls at me and gestures to Kade for another round. "I mean like here. We need to have a friends and family night or something. Get all the regulars to bring everyone they know so we can meet more quality people."

I snort a laugh. "Sounds more like a barbecue social."

He pauses, bottle halfway to his lips. "I could go for some barbecue, too."

I laugh again because of course, he could. Like most pro athletes, myself included, Tucker loves his food. Even though he's not a Texan, he sure has taken to the brisket like one. About every six months, I have to talk him down from buying a portable smoker for tailgating. The man has never gone to a tailgating party in his life and I've seen his barbecue skills. Add a truck with a tank full of gas and it's asking for an explosion. And not the good kind.

"Speaking of food," he continues because of course, he does. "What are you going to want to eat after the surgery tomorrow? Chicken noodle soup or maybe tomato with a grilled cheese?"

I've actually spent a couple of days creating a few meals and sticking them in my freezer so I won't have to cook for a while. I'm not thrilled about the idea of not eating everything totally fresh, but it's better than surviving off fast food for the next three months. And it beats the hell out of Tucker's cooking skills.

"I'm having surgery not contracting the flu, grandma."

"Listen, just because you'll be sleeping your day away tomorrow doesn't mean the rest of us will. I'm trying to plan ahead so I know what to feed us once you're home."

I shrug, completely indifferent to tomorrow's menu. "Just make whatever you want. If I'm hungry, I'll eat but who knows how it's gonna go. Don't wait on me."

"Oh, I wasn't planning on it. But now that you've mentioned barbecue, I may have to stop at that great little joint over by the rink on our way back from the hospital. Their smoked sausage is amazing. I wonder if they would sell me their recipe."

I'm about to give him his bi-yearly reminder of why him smoking anything is a bad idea when the door opens and Ellery walks in. Only this isn't the Ellery I know. This Ellery is sporting a shorter haircut that shows off her elegant neck.

I'm completely transfixed as I watch her rush to the bar before stopping in front of her girlfriends, who are causing a ruckus in response to the big reveal, and twirling around to show them her new cut.

She doesn't just look stunning, she also looks excited. The way she's carrying herself exudes confidence and poise. She's owning it.

Before I even know what's happening, I approach the bar. "Another something, Nicole," I say holding up my bottle, having no idea what I was drinking. Everything before now is a blur, my eyes not able to leave the sight of the beautiful woman next to me.

Immediately upon hearing my voice, Ellery turns away

from her friends to make eye contact with me, biting her lip like she's nervous.

"You don't like it," she finally squeaks out after several seconds of silence.

I do. I really do. But I also remember the conversations we've had over the last couple of weeks and I don't want my thoughts to change the way she feels about herself. I'm not the important one in this scenario.

"It doesn't matter if I like it. Do you like it?"

She hesitates, my opinion more important to her than she wants to admit. But I see it in her eyes. The beginnings of the fearless person I know she wants to be. And part of that boldness means being truthful to herself no matter what anyone else thinks. Me included.

"I do." The smile that crosses her face with that admission practically glows. "I really like it. I think with the color and the makeup, I look like a new person. A take-charge person." Her face blushes prettily and she looks down before peeking up at me through her lashes. "Fake it until I make it right?"

"There's no faking it. You're perfect the way you are."

I ignore Nicole and Lauren making "awwwww" noises behind her, although briefly, I wonder why Kiersten isn't here tonight before my attention goes back where it belongs. On Ellery.

I approach her and run the back of my hand down her soft cheek. "For the record, I love it. It gives me easy access to your neck." I lean in closer and run my nose just under her jaw making her shiver.

"Holy shit, I think I just got pregnant watching this," Lauren says making me chuckle, but I've got more important things on my mind.

"Wanna come home with me tonight?"

"You better say yes before he takes you on this bar," Lauren interrupts.

Ellery giggles then nods and I grab her hand.

"Nicole, Tucker will close out my tab."

"Hey!" I hear him yell in protest, but he deserves it for the number of times he's done the same to me.

Nicole waves me off knowing I'm a man on a mission and if Tucker doesn't pay up, I will next time I'm in. It's not like they don't all know where to find me.

Racing to the car, I have to remind myself to slow my steps so I don't drag Ellery through the parking lot.

"Sorry," I say as I hold back some of the pent-up energy I'm feeling. "I forgot you were wearing heels and can't run as fast as me."

She laughs and I'm struck by how much I enjoy the sound of her happiness. It's a stark contrast to the first time we met and something I want to hear more of.

"Heels and gravel definitely don't mix but I'm pretty sure my shoes don't matter. Your legs are twice the length of mine anyway."

I turn toward my truck before remembering her car is here.

"Mind if I drive? I can bring you back to get your car first thing in the morning."

"Sounds perfect."

As soon as my truck door is open, I hike her up and onto the seat. Before I can close the door, Ellery grabs me by the shirt and pulls me to her.

"I know you're ready to go, but I'm not sure I can wait that long."

With her words, I'm a goner. She fuses her lips to mine, kissing me hard and passionately. Ellery takes complete control as she licks the seam of my lips demanding entrance. From that second on, there's no holding back.

My arms wrap around her small body and somehow her skirt hikes up over her hips, enough to allow her legs to wrap around my waist. I can't stop myself from grinding against her, the friction doing nothing to relieve the tension that's coiling inside me.

Ellery's hips begin moving, chasing a release that won't come in this position and with this many clothes on. Neither one of us seem to care, though, too immersed in our passionate make-out session.

It isn't until I hear some catcalls from people walking into the bar that I can finally break away from her.

"I don't want to take you in the front seat of my truck in front of all our friends. We need to get home. Now." My voice is deeper and raspier than normal, thick with desire. I have never needed a woman like I need her before. And somehow I know I'll never need anyone else again.

With one last kiss, Ellery pulls away. "Let's go."

The drive to my place is only minutes but seems like it takes forever. And Ellery is awfully quiet.

Looking back and forth between her and the road, I try to figure out the look on her face. She seems deep in thought, but I can't tell if it's a dirty thought. I hope it is. "What?"

She glances up, seemingly startled by my question. "*What* what?"

I smile at her cuteness. She may look like a bombshell, but she's still the same sweet inexperienced woman I enjoy getting to know. "You're thinking too hard."

She bites her lip and I know she has something on her mind. I only hope she's not reconsidering.

"I want to do something but I'm not sure I should."

Now I'm really curious. "What is it?"

She pauses before saying, "This." Reaching over tentatively, she places her hand on my cock and begins to rub.

I hiss and make a concentrated effort to not stomp on the gas. "You should definitely do this."

"Really?"

My nostrils flare and my hips begin moving again as she strokes gently over my jeans.

"I wish my hand was underneath your clothes right now," she whispers.

I immediately go into action, unzipping my jeans and shoving my briefs aside putting her hand exactly where I want it. The relief I feel when she grasps me only lasts a second before the need to be inside her takes over again.

Ellery strokes and rubs and plays, exploring me with a gentleness that both feels amazing and leaves me wanting more. Needing more.

"It's so soft," Ellery says quietly and I almost come from the sound of her innocence.

"You seem surprised," I say more to keep myself under control than to make conversation.

"I am. I know we had sex before, but I guess I didn't really take the time to get to know this part of you."

Before I know what's happening, she leans over and kisses the tip of my cock, making my hips buck.

"Holy shit, Ellery. Honey, you need to wait to do that." She sits back up, confusion written all over her face. "I am so amped up, I'll be done before we get to my driveway if your mouth gets anywhere near my cock again."

"Your cock? That's what you call it?"

Holy shit, this woman is going to kill me with all this innocence. But I still can't help myself than to play along.

"Say it again."

Ellery licks her bright red lips. "Cock."

I groan in frustration that we're not already at my house, which seems to delight her. We both know she has total control over me in this moment. Exactly how it should be.

The last part of the drive is sweet torture as she continues to play and by the time I park in my driveway, I'm about to go out of my mind with lust.

Not bothering to fix my pants, I doubt my neighbors are paying much attention, I slide Ellery across the seat and wrap her legs around me so I can carry her into my house without breaking our connection.

"Wait!" she calls out before I've taken more than half a dozen steps. "You forgot to close up the truck."

Cursing under my breath just makes her giggle as I backtrack and shut the door.

"A little anxious are you?" Her voice is husky as she kisses down the side of my neck, nipping at the juncture of my shoulder.

"You're such a temptress."

We finally make it into my house and out of the public eye. Pushing her up against the back of the door, I revel in her groan at the contact.

"You're ready for me now, aren't you? Should I just slide your panties to the side and fuck you right here?"

She gasps as I do just that, sliding one finger and then two inside her, pumping along with her as she rides my hand. Her beautiful mouth falls open as she puffs out her breaths, unable to control herself anymore.

In seconds, I feel the walls around my fingers contract. Ellery's head falls back as she cries out her pleasure. It's possibly the most beautiful thing I've ever seen.

I keep stroking her gently as she comes down off her high, watching her every expression as she does. When her glassy eyes find mine, she says the last words I expect to hear in this moment.

"Bed. Now."

FIFTEEN
Ellery

I t feels like only seconds from my orgasm against the door, which was a pleasant surprise, until I'm lying on my back on Liam's bed watching as he gets undressed.

I could be making myself useful and taking off my own clothes, but I can't stop staring at him.

He's a giant compared to almost anyone I've ever known before, but there's such a gentleness about him when he's with me. His bulky frame is defined by abs that could rival that of a Greek god. And his shoulders, good lord they're broad and massive and the sight of them makes me want to climb him like a tree. Which wouldn't be too far-fetched considering our height difference.

Liam doesn't seem to care that I'm on the shorter side. If anything, he seems to like picking me up and tossing me around in the bedroom. I don't mind it at all. It gives me a strange sense of vulnerability when I'm with him, but in a good way. Like he can shield me from the harshness of the outside world. It's not something I've ever really felt before so it's not unwelcome.

As his boxer briefs slide down his legs joining the rest of his clothes, his eyes catch mine and he gives me a shy smile. "What?"

"I'm just admiring your physique," I answer honestly. There's no reason to lie. He knows he's sexy.

"I'd like to admire yours, too. You planning on getting naked?"

He slides his hand up and down his cock and the side of his lips tilt up as he waits for my answer.

"I was hoping you could get me naked."

His nostrils flare as he stalks toward me, his hand still stroking.

This is the sexiest thing I've ever seen. Not that I have much experience in that department. But something about the tightly restrained power behind all his movements makes all of my inhibitions disappear.

I want this man in every way I can get him.

Kneeling before me, Liam grabs me by my ankle and pulls it to his lips. I groan at the contact as he nips while removing my strappy sandals. Who knew this was an erogenous zone? Obviously him.

Once my shoes are discarded, he slides his big hands up my legs but he doesn't go for my skirt, he goes under it grabbing my panties and pulling them down, down, down, so slowly I want to scream. When my panties are finally over my feet and on the floor, he spreads me wide and just stares at my most intimate spot.

Showing me his phone, his eyebrows raise just slightly. "May I?"

I feel my eyes widen in surprise. I find his question a huge turn-on, but am I brave enough to let him take a picture of me like this?

"Wha… um… what are you going to do with it?"

"Look at it. Probably jack off to it when you aren't here."

My breathing hitches at the idea that a simple picture of me could turn him on so much.

Quickly, I nod. "But I want to see it."

He smiles his agreement and moves the phone into position. I feel myself getting even more turned on just knowing what he's doing.

"Holy fuck," he groans and I hear the click of the camera.

Turning the phone around like I asked, all I see is me. Not my face or any recognizable part of me. The part that only Liam will recognize. I'm swollen and glistening and while it doesn't do anything to turn me on, I suddenly understand the appeal it has for Liam.

"Do you want me to delete it?"

I shake my head slowly, unable to stop myself from biting my lip. "I want you to look at it whenever I'm not here and you need to take the edge off on your own."

Liam's eyes roll in the back of his head and he lets out a groan before tossing the phone aside and attacking me with his mouth. He's brutal as he licks and nips and feasts on me like a starving man. It's all I can do to not grab him by the hair and hold him in place so we can stay like this forever.

All too soon, Liam is kissing up my body, pulling off the rest of my clothes as he goes, until he's lying on top of me. But this is not what I had in mind.

Pushing him back, I try for confidence when I demand, "Roll over."

He grabs me and flips us until I'm impaled on top of him, my hips rolling, enjoying the feel of him inside me. Liam on the other hand is relaxing, hands behind his head like he doesn't have a care in the world. He does though. I can see the excitement in his eyes. The anticipation of what's coming. Not to mention the hardness throbbing inside me. And that's when my nerves hit.

Sensing my change in mood, Liam reaches up and cups my cheek. "What's wrong?"

"I've never done it like this before," I confess quietly.

"Never?"

I shake my head and huff out a small, humorless laugh. "Kevin liked me on the bottom."

I immediately know I've said the wrong thing when Liam sits up so quickly he pushes deeper inside me, making me gasp. "First things first, he has no place in my bedroom when you and I are being intimate. It's only you and me in here. Nothing kills the mood more than comparing what's happening between us to your former lover."

My stomach drops and I feel my cheeks flame with embarrassment. "I…I… I'm sorry. I didn't mean to make you mad."

"You didn't make me mad. I just need to be very clear on that." He gently takes my cheeks in his hands and kisses the tip of my nose. "Ellery, he lost his chance with you and I'll be damned if we need to talk about him again in regard to sex. From here on out, it's just you and me. Okay?"

I nod quickly, still feeling the sting of shame at bringing up an ex during such an intense moment.

"Second and this is the important one…"

I swallow hard, nervous about what he's going to say. He is a huge, alpha male of a man. What if I'm not enough for him?

"… don't ever be embarrassed if you want to try things with me. Want to ride me?" He pulls my hips toward him in a mini thrust. "Tell me. Want to try reverse cowgirl?

I'm game. Don't hold back. I want you to learn your likes and dislikes. What gives you maximum pleasure. And in return, when I'm in the mood to turn you around and fuck you against the wall, I'll let you know."

I feel the walls inside me clench at his words. He must feel it too because he looks down at where we're joined and smiles. "Does that make you excited? The idea of me riding you hard and making you come until you can't walk anymore?"

I can't make the words come out, so I nod instead.

He runs his hands down my chest, kneading my breasts on the way down. "Have you ever done it doggy style before?"

Still no words but another shake of my head and more movement from my hips as my thoughts go wild.

"You want to try it?"

Another nod. This time, though, Liam isn't having it.

"No way, sweets. You have to use your words. Do you want to try it doggy style?"

"Yes," I finally squeak out. "Please yes."

He picks me up like I weigh nothing and pulls out of me, making us both groan at the lost contact. Gently, he lays me on my stomach and rips my skirt off of me. His big hands grab my hips and with a quick pull, hikes my naked ass in the air. The cool air contrasts with how hot my skin feels and goose pimples cover my body.

Liam's hands rub up and down my spine, up and down my ass, fingers gently running up my slit as he lines himself up and pushes inside. Slowly, slowly he stretches me and I can't help the groan of pleasure that leaves my body.

"Liam!" I yell when he thrusts once quickly and hits a spot inside my body I never knew was there.

"You like that?" he practically whispers, body bent

over me so he can run his nose up and down my ear. "You like me taking you from behind?"

"Yes!" I practically shriek, my whole body feeling like a live wire as he continues with his small thrusts, each one building the feeling inside me.

He increases his pace and soon I can hear his hips slapping against my thighs, the sound encouraging me to sit back more so he never leaves me. Never leaves this position.

Liam grabs my hips and sits back on his knees, taking me with him so I'm sitting on top of him. He moves me back and forth, up and down, increasing the pace.

"Touch yourself," he breathes in my ear. "Reach your hand down between your legs and feel me inside you."

I do as he demands, opening my fingers so I can rub my clit with the heel of my hand while my fingers graze his cock.

"There you go, sweets. Your pussy is so sweet."

"Ooooooh," I moan, knowing I'm close, but needing something more. I just don't know what. "Liam," I plea, hoping he knows what my body needs more than I do.

"I know. I got you." Bending me forward, he gets me on my hands and knees and he thrusts. No, it's more forceful than just that. He drives into me, fast and furious. The only thing I can do is hang on for dear life as he works me over, hitting that sweet spot over and over and over until my body finally snaps.

" O O O O O H H H H H H H M M M M M - MMYYYYYYyyyyyyyyyyyyyyyyyyy………."

My voice trails off as the orgasm releases, and then I listen as Liam reaches his own climax. His body practically frozen as he groans from deep within his chest, trying to catch his breath while still making tiny little thrusts, milking out his orgasm for all it's worth.

We collapse in a heap of tangled, sweaty limbs, no words spoken. Just heavy breathing as we slowly come down from the oxytocin high.

Liam pulls me closer to him, his heavy thigh slung over my leg. He's not just the big spoon. He's the all-encompassing spoon.

"How do you feel?"

"I had no idea sex could be like that."

I feel the rumble in his chest as he chuckles. "So, I take I you enjoyed it?"

"Um, yeah. That was…" I try to think of a word to describe it but there's nothing. "Wow."

"It's always wow with you." He kisses the back of my neck and I snuggle in deeper, content to be right here as long as he'll have me. "What do you want to do now? You hungry?"

"Only for a little more… cock." I can't help the giggle that comes out when I use the term he gave me. It sounds so strange coming from my mouth. But it makes me feel worldly and experienced. Like a grown-up.

I can practically feel Liam smiling behind me. "Woman, you are going to kill me."

"Maybe. But what a way to go out."

SIXTEEN

Liam

Ellery.

She's so beautiful in the shower. Her body, so slick. Her insides so wet as I pump slowly in and out of her. Her hair slicked back.

Man, I love this haircut. It gives me easy access to all my favorite places of her.

"Ellery," I call out, hoping she's as close to coming as I am.

"Nope. Just me motherfucker."

The deep voice is in stark contrast to Ellery's normally sweet one. What's happening? Is she sick?

My desire to protect her from whatever ails her interrupts what could have been the most powerful orgasm of my life.

"There you are. I see you coming around."

I recognize that voice now. Fucking Tucker. What the fuck is he doing in the shower with me and my girl?

"Get out, asshole." My voice doesn't sound nearly as angry as I feel.

"Can't. The nurse says I have to stay right here until you're able to walk to the car."

Nurse? What nurse? And why do I have to walk to my car?

Everything begins to go fuzzy around me and Ellery suddenly disappears.

Am I dreaming? And which part? Is Ellery the dream or is Tucker? My head is fuzzy and I'm so confused.

What I assume are hands lightly slap my cheeks. That confirms it. Ellery would never do that, although I'm not sure how my brain knows that tidbit of information. Tucker would though.

I bat him away, now irritated at the intrusion on what was only a sex dream. Too bad. It was a really good one.

I only get a moment's reprieve before the hands are back, peeling my eyelids open. Now I'm really getting pissed.

"Rise and shine, lover boy, before you embarrass the sweet nurse with that woody you're popping."

I'm unconcerned with any wood I may be sporting right now. Tucker has seen my dick before. Locker rooms and all that. Still, I'm curious who all is here with me.

Finally getting my eyes to cooperate and open enough that I can get my bearings somewhat straight, I don't see the woman of my dreams like I'd hoped. Not that I thought the deep voice of my dream was hers, but it would have been nice to see her instead of the dickhead in my face.

"Nice to see you, sunshine."

I want to slap the grin right off his face.

"I may be down an arm, but I can still punch your lights out with the other one if you don't get away from me."

"Oooh. You're a cranky patient. I was wondering what you were like after anesthesia. Too bad. I was hoping for my video to go viral but no one cares about seeing someone be combative when they come to. Why can't you be one of those funny patients?"

"You're an asshole," I croak out, my mouth suddenly feeling really dry. "Water."

Tucker grabs a large white thermos style mug from the bedside table and puts the straw up to my lips while he continues to torture me with his chatter.

"The good news is the nurse has a crush on me, so she won't be paying attention to your piss poor attitude anyway."

The curtain opens just as I finish drinking and a small woman in scrubs walks in. She glances over at Tucker who of course gives her a megawatt smile.

"Good to see you both are focused on the well-being of the patient," I grumble, still unable to clear the fog from my brain.

"Don't mind him," Tucker says, never taking his eyes off the woman he's currently wooing in my time of need. "It turns out he's one of those difficult patients. Unfortunate for all of us."

She giggles and checks some monitors. "How are you feeling Mr. Tremblay?"

"Like the surgeon needs to come back in here."

She approaches my bed, her bedside manner suddenly kicking in. "Are you in pain?"

"Yes. But it's not my shoulder. Doc needs to remove the dick off that guy's head." I try to point at Tucker but my arm drops back onto the bed. I had no idea holding my hand up could be so exhausting.

Tucker shakes his head like he's offended. "See what I'm saying? His insults don't even make sense. Such a shame he's got a mean streak."

I have to give the fucker credit—he's playing this up pretty well for her benefit. I bet her number is in his phone before we leave.

Moving some wires and tubes around, she continues to flirt while getting me situated. "Believe me, we've had some combative patients before and he's not one of them. Once the anesthesia wears off, he'll be back to normal."

"How long will that take?" I ask, feeling groggy and sleepy again.

"It depends on how long it takes for your body to burn it all off." Placing her hand on my arm, she finally looks at me instead of my asshole friend. "Do you need anything?"

I try and fail to shake my head, my eyes feeling heavy.

"Go back to sleep then," she says kindly. "There's no rush."

I drift off, barely registering Tucker ask my nurse if she's free tonight…

• • •

I startle awake, a searing pain in my shoulder.

"Fuuuuuck," I groan as I try to situate myself on my couch using only one arm. It's not as easy as it sounds, especially with Patches laying on my chest.

When it becomes obvious his pillow is trying to sit up, he drops to the floor with an irritated flick of his tail.

The smell of food makes my stomach protest loudly at the fact that my last meal was before midnight last night. I have no idea how long it's been since I've eaten. I also don't know how I even got here.

"Are you finally up for good?" I glance over to see Tucker looking awfully relaxed on my other couch. His feet are kicked up while he chows down on a giant plastic bowl full of cereal.

"Are you eating my food?"

His eyes stay glued to Sports Center on my big screen. "You've been out for a long time. I've had to entertain myself all day and I got hungry."

"What am I smelling?"

"Lunch. Fish tacos. You know how the smell lingers forever."

My stomach rumbles again. "You ate them all, didn't you?"

A drop of milk slides down his chin. He uses the collar of his shirt to wipe it off like a freaking neanderthal. "I did you a favor. They're no good reheated."

Still trying to sit up, I move the wrong way and hiss in a breath at the pain that shoots through my shoulder. It radiates all the way down into my arm.

"Need a pain killer?" Tucker puts the bowl down and grabs a bottle of pills off the coffee table. "Doctor prescribed some good stuff if you want it."

I shake my head, careful not to move too much. "Nah. I'd rather use something over the counter if I can. Do I have any ibuprofen?"

"Always the martyr." He sighs with resolve, like his opinion even matters. Considering what I'm wanting is also on the coffee table, his words don't hold much bite. "Four okay?"

"Yep."

To his credit, Tucker doesn't complain about doing menial tasks like refilling that giant mug from the hospital with cold water and bringing everything to me. This is why he's such a good buddy. He likes to talk shit, but none of it is serious. It's just his humor. When it really comes down to it, Tucker is loyal to a fault and one of the most reliable people I know when he cares about someone.

I swallow the meds down like a good little patient and once I'm finally sitting upright, keep hold of my water. There's no doubt I'm slightly dehydrated. Or maybe it's the last of the anesthesia making me feel like I have cottonmouth.

The sun is shining in through the windows so I know it's well into the day, but I can't figure out by how much. "How long have I been out?"

"Dude. Literally all day. I was hoping you'd be up by dinnertime because I'm starving again."

I'm surprised by his comment. "Is it really that late?"

He glances at his phone. "Yep. Five thirty on the dot."

"Holy shit." I rub my hand down my face and sure enough, my afternoon stubble has grown in. I can't believe I've slept all day. I'm still in some pain but at least my mind finally seems clear. Enough that I know there are holes in my memory now. "How did we get here anyway?"

Tucker looks at me with surprise. "You don't remember?"

"Last thing I can recall, you were flirting with a cute nurse who was ignoring my pain because she was having too much fun with you."

"Ah, the lovely Alisa." Tucker grins but I'm not sure if it's the shit-eating kind or if hearts should be coming out of his eyes. "She was a nice specimen, wasn't she?"

"I love how you threw in a big word because it sounds science-y," I retort with a roll of my eyes.

"It was good, right?"

"Not at all. Answer my question, dude. When did we get back?"

"Oh yeah," he says, getting back on track. "Right before lunch. It was quite an adventure."

"I'm hinting a little sarcasm in your tone."

"Not a little. A lot. It took like two hours for you to finally wake up, but since you don't remember anything, maybe you were just sleepwalking."

"I didn't make an ass out of myself did I?"

He shrugs. "Nothing you need to send flowers for. Just your normal asshole demeanor. But don't worry. I used it to my advantage."

"I don't think I want to know," I mutter with a shake of my head. No telling how he threw me under the bus for his own personal entertainment.

"Alisa felt bad for how much of your shit I have to put up with that she made sure I had her number before we left. So, thank you for that. We already have plans on her next day off."

I don't bother responding. I could be mad but if it weren't for my interest in one particular pixie, I'd probably have done the same thing if roles were reversed.

"Anyway, you up for some grub?"

My stomach growls in response. "What are you cooking? Make double for me."

"Pfft." He begins scrolling through his phone. "I'm cooking nothing for you. We're getting something delivered."

"That takes forever. Just do pick up."

"And leave your invalid ass? I don't think so."

The doorbell suddenly rings stopping the conversation. Tucker's brows furrow. "Are you expecting someone?"

I shake my head, just as confused as he is. "No."

Tucker tosses the remote to me. "Here. I've watched the highlight reel too many times to count already. Make yourself useful and find something else for us to watch while I get rid of whoever is interrupting guys' day."

"Is that what you're calling today? Guys' day? Not recovering from surgery day?"

"It sounds better. Your grumpy ass could use some mind over matter," he calls over his shoulder.

I close my eyes and blow out a breath as more pain shoots through my shoulder. I expected today to be hard but that doesn't make it any less painful. This sucks.

Eventually, the throbbing subsides a bit and I'm able to flip on the guide to figure out what's on. All of a sudden Tucker calls out.

"Hot dog! Ask and you shall receive!"

"What are you going on about?" I ask as he comes back into the room carrying some bags.

"Someone anticipated our every need and sent food over." He carefully drops the bags on the coffee table and begins digging through them. "Man, I love Jason's Deli. Check it out." He pulls a large covered bowl out and peels the top open. "Broccoli and Cheese Soup. This stuff is amazing. Are these cat treats?"

"Who sent it?"

He tosses the cat treats aside and digs for more food. "No idea, but we're going to eat good tonight."

My phone vibrates on the table and I lean forward gingerly to grab it, trying not to put any stress on my shoulder. Easier said than done.

I've got half a dozen text messages, mostly from my mom and sisters checking on me. But the one at the top is what catches my eye. It's from Ellery.

Ellery: I wasn't sure how you were feeling so I sent over some soup. It's on your front porch. If you're hungry, there are a couple of muffulettas in there, too. Patches has some dessert in there, too. Hope you're

not in too much pain. Let me know if you need anything. ☺

I immediately dismiss the idea of texting her back. Not with one working hand and especially not after a nice surprise like this one. Pressing the call button, I ignore Tucker as he continues to give commentary while he rummages.

"Liam?"

Her voice immediately brightens my shitty day.

"Thank you for the food. And the stuff for Patches. You didn't have to do that."

"Feel free to do it any time!" Tucker yells.

I try to kick him with my foot to get him to shut up but he dodges me.

"Oh good. I'm glad someone is there with you."

I can't help but smile at her concern for my well-being. "Don't be too glad. It's Tucker and he's been eating my food and using up my amenities all day."

"Last time I hold a barf bag up to your face when you're threatening to hurl in the recovery room," he grumbles, snatching the remote back and dropping down on the couch with a huge sandwich in his hand.

Ellery laughs on the other end of the call. "How long is he staying?"

"No idea. I'm sure he'll stick around as long as there's food."

Tucker nods and raises the sandwich indicating I've nailed it.

"Did you ever hire a night nurse to help you for the next few days?"

"I didn't," I admit. "Time got away from me and it feels so unnecessary to have someone here if all I'm going to be doing is sleeping anyway. I'll just put some ibuprofen next to my bed before I crash for the night. Unless you want to come be my night nurse."

I'm joking with her, but the phone goes silent.

Crap. Did that sound pushy? Last thing I want to do is make her feel uncomfortable. Quickly, I try to figure out a way to backtrack without sticking my foot even more in my mouth.

She beats me to it.

"I know you're joking, but it would make me feel better if you'd let me do that."

That is not the response I was expecting.

"Really?"

"Yeah. I know you're a grown man and all, but what if your sutures get infected or you come down with a fever or there's a fire or something. I would feel so much better if you had help. And I can sleep on the couch," she tosses in. "That doesn't bother me. I just don't want you to be alone until you're a little more settled."

I can almost hear her biting her lip with nervousness from sharing how she really feels. She has nothing to be shy about, though. I love when she tells me how she really feels.

"There's no reason for you to sleep on the couch. My bed is big enough for both of us."

Tucker's eyebrows rise and he stops chewing. I wave him off hoping he'll take the hint to get out and give me some privacy but as expected, he ignores me.

"I promise I'm not trying to wedge my way into your home," Ellery says. "I'll just worry about you otherwise."

A warmth runs through me at her words. I have friends and family that love me but it's different with Ellery. Knowing she cares about my health and well-being, and not my hockey stats or bank account, is a new kind of feeling. It's not unexpected. Ellery isn't even close to being a hockey fan so I know that has nothing to do with why she likes me. But knowing she cares about the guy off the ice makes this shitty situation the tiniest bit easier to bear.

"El, you can wedge your way into my home any time you want."

Tucker fake coughs and says, "Pussy whipped," then fake coughs again. Thankfully I have a pill bottle next to me that I launch at his head. Unfortunately, I only have one hand to both hold the phone and throw so I miss.

"What time will you be here? I'll make sure Tucker is long gone by then."

He flips me the bird but I ignore him.

"I have about an hour's worth of work left and then I need to swing by my place to grab clothes."

"Bring enough for several nights. I may get really sick and need you here with me."

I hear a small gasp and then quiet laughter. "I'll see what I can do. Tell Tucker to stick around for a couple of hours and I'll see you soon."

"Sounds good."

We say our goodbyes and I toss the phone down next to me, not wanting to respond to my family just yet. I need to sit in my sudden good mood for a bit before the reality of my injury hits again.

Tucker crumples up his trash and mutters, "Puuuuuusssyyyyyy whipped," again.

I just smile and ignore him. He can call me whatever he wants. The woman I have literal dreams about is coming to take care of me. If that makes me whipped, I kind of like it.

SEVENTEEN
Ellery

I spend two nights with Liam, keeping a close eye on his sutures and his temperature. I know I'm overthinking, but a friend of mine had a post-surgery infection once and had to go back under the knife to clean the injury out. I'll never forget how ugly the scar ended up being or how painful she said it was. I don't want that for Liam. I care a lot. I care too much, actually.

Logically, I know my feelings should scare me—it's too much too soon. If I think too hard about it, I can feel my insecurities start to set in. But being with Liam is just… easy, so I find myself not getting too much in my own head. But how can I not? Liam is interested in my thoughts and feelings like I'm interested in his. We don't always agree, but we both enjoy listening to opposing thoughts which is so different than my previous relationship. It makes me feel valued in a way I never have before. And he doesn't mind my overbearing ways, which is a plus.

It also helps that the sex is amazing. Not that we'll be doing that anytime soon. Liam has a long road ahead of him and I don't want to risk his career for a few seconds of pleasure. No matter how amazing it may be.

I wanted to stay with him longer, but Tucker had already agreed to hang out for the weekend to keep an eye on Liam, and I had already promised my parents I'd come for a visit. They're my favorite people in the world and it's been too long since I've seen them.

I'm really nervous about our visit this time. They still don't about my lavender pixie cut or that I treated myself to a second ear piercing the other day. What are they going to say about my new look? And the new me?

I was *this close* to coming up with an excuse to bail out, but with everything squared away in Liam's world, there was no real reason to cancel. Besides, I have to show my parents the updated version of myself eventually. I might as well get it out of the way before the holidays. This will give them several months to get used to my new fashion statements before the extended family gets ahold of me. I don't even want to think about how my judgy Aunt Nelda will respond.

Driving into the short driveway that leads to a small two-story yellow home, I take my last few deep breaths.

"Relax, Ellery," I say to myself. "They love you no matter what you look like. And if they don't, hair always grows back."

A strangled laugh comes out of me as I think of how long it would take for my hair to be that length again. The color would be easy to change but the length would take years, probably. I wonder if Jayden could recommend something to help it grow faster.

No. I don't need to be thinking like that. I like my hair and that's what matters.

One last deep breath and I open the door before I freak

myself out more and accidentally restart my car and drive away.

Leaving my suitcase in the backseat to get later, I grab my purse and make my way up the small walkway to the front door. I don't even make it all the way up the steps before the door flings open, my mom racing outside to greet me.

"Oh sweetie, it's so good to see you." She hugs me, holding me tightly and I feel my shoulders begin to relax. There's just something about my mother's hugs that make everything right with the world.

I'm sure being an only child and a late-in-life baby is part of why we're so close. I've heard all the stories about being a miracle baby to a couple who had given up on having a child.

That's part of why my parents have always been great. They came to every gymnastics meet. They volunteered on the PTA. They worked behind the scenes for school programs. And they always did it with a smile on their faces. By contrast, I saw way too many moms also volunteer, but complain the whole time. It always seemed strange to me. Mine were always happily involved and other moms just weren't.

In hindsight, I think those other moms were probably raising multiple kids, some of them on their own, and just trying to make it through the days. My parents, on the other hand, were at an age where they seemed much more chill and were able to let insignificant things go and enjoy the journey. They're still that way.

Mom pulls away much too soon and looks me up and down. "That haircut! You are so glamorous. Are you sure you don't live in New York City?"

"You like it?" I ask as I mess with the small hairs on

the back of my head, trying to flatten them out even though they're fine.

"I do. I never would have guessed something this short would look great on you, but you know me. I can't visualize most things. This is why I work with numbers and not colors."

She links our arms together, dragging me into the house and out of the heat and humidity.

"I was shocked at first," I admit as we walk through the small living room into the kitchen where we all typically gather. "Thank goodness for apps that let you try out hairstyles first."

"I didn't know that was a thing." She grabs a glass out of the cabinet to get me some water. She does it every time someone comes over. She doesn't offer, just does. I love that about her. "You should show me how to use it. I've had this bun for way too long. I pine for the days when I had poofy bangs and multicolored lashes."

I furrow my brows and run through my memories, but I have no recollection of what she's talking about. "Wait... what? When did you have that?"

Mom hands me my water and sits down. "Long before you were born. You know this. We've told you stories."

"Uh... I'm pretty sure you haven't. I would have remembered."

She thinks for a moment, confusion written all over her face. "Well, who did we talk to about this? Have you never seen the picture of the night your dad and I met?"

My hands go palms up and I shrug one shoulder. "I don't know. Maybe?"

Mom laughs lightly. "Oh, dear. You would remember if you had. Come with me to the living room. Have I got a story for you."

Abandoning our waters on the kitchen table, we head to the living room where I relax onto the couch we've had since I was a child. It's old and frayed in places. But it's also the most comfortable place in the house according to me. I watch as mom runs her fingers over the spines of several books on the shelf before pulling out the one she wants.

"Here it is." When she opens it and begins rifling through things, I realize it's not a real book. The inside is hollow and contains a bunch of pictures. No wonder I never saw it before. I never tried to read that book before.

Finding what she wants, Mom hands me a picture and my jaw drops.

"That's *Dad*?"

"The one and only," she says with an amused grin.

"But... he has a mohawk." I look between her and the picture several times. "A spiky one."

"Of course, he does. It was the 80's. You wouldn't dare go see The Ramones in concert with your hair down."

The Ramones part doesn't surprise me. They've always been music lovers. The hair, however, is a shock to my system.

I blink rapidly, still unable to wrap my mind around what I'm seeing. "But dad's an accountant. They would never let him go to work looking like this."

"Oh no. Never. During work hours he kept his hair down. His boss still didn't like it. Called him a grown-up hippie, but it wasn't against company policy so there was nothing he could do. At night, when we went out, your dad would grab the Dippity Do and Aqua Net, secure that puppy as high as he could get it, and use whatever temporary spray color he was in the mood for. That night I guess it was purple."

I'm having a hard time wrapping my brain around all this. Especially since she has a dreamy look on her face. My mother. The most conservative dresser I know was gaga over a guy with spiky purple hair and charcoal eyeliner. I almost pinch myself to see if I'm dreaming.

"I'm sorry. I've… I'm still…" at a loss for words. "I have never seen him like this. Not even on Halloween."

She pats my hand gently. "Honey, you were a late-in-life baby. You came along right when grunge was the thing and neither of us enjoyed that music phase at all. Thanks for giving us an out from those concerts by the way. Perfect timing on your part."

I giggle. Sometimes I forget what a wry sense of humor my mom has.

"By the time that era was over and we could get on board with the musical fashion of the day again, you were in the gym five to six nights a week, sometimes until late, and we were driving you across the state to meets every weekend. We were too tired to get back into the music and concert scene."

"It's just so weird to think of you and dad out partying like that."

"You think that's strange… do you recognize the woman next to him?"

I look at the picture a little closer before I squeal, "Is that *you*?"

"Thirty-five years younger and forty pounds lighter," she says with a giant smile.

Sure enough, my very youthful-looking mother is sporting bangs almost as high as my dad's mohawk. She's got one lace glove on and a see-through net shirt with a green bra underneath. I don't think I can ever look at my responsible, strait-laced parents the same way again.

"This was at our very first Ramones concert," she boasts. "We had mutual friends who wanted to go and they introduced us. The rest is history."

"A history I have no knowledge of, apparently."

"Not on purpose. I honestly thought you knew and just didn't care."

"No, I had no idea. I would have worried a lot less about you seeing my hair if I'd known about this. A lavender pixie cut is nothing compared to your giant feathered do."

"Oh honey," she says gently. "You were worried about us seeing your new style?"

I look up at her and see she's morphed into concerned mom mode. This is the expression she would always give me when I had heavy things on my mind that I needed to talk out with someone I trusted. Words start tumbling out of my mouth before I can stop them.

"It's not just the haircut. It's the makeup and the break-up. There's just so much happening and I feel like I'm becoming this new person. I like it, but I guess I'm afraid you won't like the new me."

She settles in a little, making sure to look me in the eye. "Let me ask you a question. Is the new you still kind and hard working. And maybe cares about people a bit too much?"

"Of course, Mom. Those things don't change just because I look different."

"Exactly." She grabs my chin and leans in close. "You are still the same girl I know and love. The rest is just packaging."

"I know that. I just get mixed reviews on everything right now."

"How so?"

"My friends seem to love the new look. My job, my boss, Kevin, they seem to think I've lost my mind."

My mother harumphs, lips pressed together in a hard line. "I'm not inclined to believe Kevin, or his mother, have an opinion that really matters right now."

I hold back a smile, recognizing her mama bear instincts are kicking in. She didn't take the news of our break-up well. Not that the relationship ended, but the how and why of it all. "Are you still upset about the way Kevin dumped me?"

She sniffs and turns away. "I'm saying he lost his right to have a say in any part of your life the minute he took his mother's advice and cast you aside. But that's neither here nor there anymore." She slaps my leg lightly, her mood shifting as fast as the conversation. "Tell me what else is going on with you."

I bite my lip, wanting to spill the beans about Liam but afraid of doing it right on the heels of her displeasure with my last relationship. I don't even know if I'm in a relationship right now. Sex and hanging out doesn't always constitute a commitment.

Still, I want her to be included in the good things that are happening in my life, and Liam is a good thing. I decide to bite the bullet and see what happens.

"I met a man."

Her eyes widen. "A man? What kind of man are we talking about?"

"What?"

"When you told me about Kevin you mentioned another guy. The word man sounds very…"

"…alpha. I know. But he's a professional hockey player and he's huge next to me so man sounds right."

"Is he kind to you?"

M.E. CARTER

I think back to the other night when his tongue was between my legs. Kind is an understatement. I don't think my mother would appreciate that information, though.

"He is. He wants to hear my opinions on things and supports me when I make decisions like chopping off all my hair. He's just… so much more than I had with Kevin. And it's only been a short amount of time."

"Can I be honest?"

"Sure."

"I always knew you'd outgrow Kevin. I think he knew it too."

This is surprising. Neither of my parents ever said anything about it before. "Really?"

"The benefit of being born to older parents is you were the only child in the room most of the time," she explains. "You modeled your behavior after adults, while developing and expressing opinions of your own. You could hold your own about current events by the time you were ten. It's one of the reasons you're such an asset at your job. You know how to adjust to almost any situation.

"Kevin on the other hand, wasn't raised to have his own thought processes. He's stuck where he's at because this was all he was supposed to be—a young man who was groomed to take over his family's business at some point and to stay close to the hive."

"You don't think I'm staying close to the hive?"

"I think you're your own person who has never had the chance to explore very far into the world. The *curse* of being born to older parents is that we're much more conservative. Not necessarily in our views, but in trends and technology, things like that. In some ways, we weren't able to introduce you to that side of life so you're a little behind in knowing how parts of the world work."

"You make it sound like I'm immature."

"Quite the contrary. You're almost too mature. It's served you well, but now you're finding another side of yourself. It seems to me that you're finding out you're trendier than you realized. Maybe you have an interest in makeup you never knew was there. There's nothing wrong with that."

If she only knew the other things I'm exploring.

"I think it might be time to get a new job."

It's the first time I've admitted that out loud and oddly, it doesn't sound wrong.

Mom just smiles. "I was waiting for you to come to that conclusion. Like I said, you outgrew Kevin and you outgrew his family."

I crinkle my nose and admit the other part of it all. "I'm kind of scared."

"Good. Nothing good ever came from staying stagnant. Take a chance. Life should be an adventure. Besides, you're young enough to fail. Do it now, when no one else is depending on you. Take the chances you'll never get to take again."

"Thanks, Mom."

She leans over and wraps me in her arms. "Always, baby. You're the love of my life. Even with lavender hair."

EIGHTEEN
Liam

It's been two weeks since my surgery. Probably the longest two weeks of my life. I've been stuck in this sling and haven't been allowed to start physical therapy so I've been sitting on my ass all day every day watching television and feeling antsy. It sucks.

The sutures finally came out today and I was cleared to start squeezing a ball to build my muscles back up.

Yup. I've gone from hours on the ice every day, doing drills, shooting pucks, dodging opponents, and slamming into walls to squeezing. A fucking. Ball.

Irritated with the situation, I try to rear back and throw the damn thing across the room, but a searing pain shoots through my shoulder when I pull too far and the ball just ends up in my lap.

Hearing my hiss, Ellery's eyes leave her laptop and glance over at me. "Careful. It's only day one of PT."

I sigh in frustration. Bored out of my mind, I look over at what she's doing. Anything is better than yet another episode of Queer Eye at this point.

"What are you working on?"

"My resume."

That grabs my attention. "Yeah? You need a new job?"

She opens her mouth to speak but closes it quickly and bites her lip.

"What?"

"Your number one rule is that *his* name doesn't come up but I can't tell you without saying it."

"My number one rule is not saying his name when I'm inside you, not when we're sitting on the couch in sweats," I clarify.

"Oh." She looks genuinely surprised which amuses me more than it probably should. My boredom must seriously be off the charts if I'm encouraging her to talk about her ex. "Well in that case—I don't want to work for his family anymore. I don't think his mom is as nice as she pretends to be and I'm ready for something new."

I nod in understanding. "Solid plan. How'd you end up working there anyway?"

She leans forward and gently places her laptop on the coffee table before settling back against the cushions. "I guess because I was dating Kevin and they needed someone to fill that position. Seemed like a win/win at the time."

"And now?"

She purses her lips. "Now I can't help but wonder if the next girl he dates will get my job."

"Oof. That's rough. You really think that would happen?"

"I don't know. But there's nothing holding me there so I don't really want to find out."

I think for a second as I run through the list of people I know. I meet people from all backgrounds of life regularly and some of them are great people. Surely one of them would know of an opening that could fit Ellery's skillset. In fact, I vaguely remember hearing something the other day.

"Have you applied at the administrative offices of the Slingers?"

"Your team's office?"

"Yeah. Why not? I happen to know they have a position like that open right now."

"A position like what?"

This is where my knowledge runs out. "Accounting or data or, I don't know. It has something to do with numbers."

Ellery laughs. "So maybe a cashier in food service?"

I pinch her ribs making her squeal, then pull her until she's straddling me. She has to help me out, but the end result is still the same. "That's enough out of you, smartass."

She opens her legs wider, connecting us right where I want, she grinds her sweet spot into me making us both groan. My lips immediately find hers for a passionate kiss, but I have more questions I want answers to.

Pulling back, I can't help but admire how her lips are already a bit swollen from me. "What else have you always wanted to try but didn't?"

"What do you mean?"

I smooth out the cute little furrow between her brows. "Well, you colored your hair, then you got some red lipstick."

"You like when I wear my red lipstick."

"I like you wearing it and wrapping those red lips around my cock."

She smacks my good arm, but I barely feel it with how tiny she is.

"Then you cut your hair. What else do you want to

try?"

She thinks and a blush creeps up her face. Now I'm really intrigued.

"What?" I encourage with a quick squeeze to her rear.

"I sort of made a to-do list. Like a bucket list but not quite as extravagant."

"Oooooh. What's on that list? Anything sexual?"

She giggles and I can't help but enjoy seeing the smile on her face. Her being here with me is the only thing keeping me in a halfway decent mood.

"You're the idea man on anything in the bedroom."

"Damn straight, baby."

She runs her fingers through my hair, not making eye contact so I know she's fighting her nerves. But to her credit, she finally spills the tea.

"I've always thought about getting a tattoo."

I'm surprised by her admission, but less so than she probably thinks. "Now we're talking. What kind of tattoo? Where do you want it?"

She twists her lips, clearly embarrassed to tell me.

"Don't be shy. Tell me."

"A rib tattoo."

I pull the hem of her shirt up and inspect that part of her body. Her skin is smooth and creamy—a perfect canvas for some art. I really want to be there when she takes this leap.

Smirking at her, I decide tonight is the night. "So, let's go."

Her eyes widen in surprise. "What, now?"

"Why not? I don't have anything better to do unless you count sitting here squeezing a damn ball. You have big plans or something?"

She bites her bottom lip and I can practically see the

cogs turning in her brain. I raise my eyebrows in question, waiting for her answer.

Finally, she smiles and I know she's getting some ink tonight.

"Fine," she says haughtily. "Let's do it."

• • •

"How are you holding up?"

Ellery breathes out slowly, tightly gripping my hand. "It doesn't tickle. It kind of feels like tiny little rips from bar work. Only instead of it being on my hands, it's on my side."

"I have no idea what that means."

She starts to giggle but thinks better of it while there's a man with a needle gun hovering over her. "Rips. When the callouses on your palms rip from swinging around the bar too many times."

"Ouch," I say with a grimace. "That sounds painful."

"You get used to it after a while. Just spray some throat spray on it to take the edge off and get back to work."

"They make you get back up on the bars when you're bleeding like that? Doesn't it take forever to heal?"

"They never really do. Unless you get lucky and have a couple of days off of that event."

I shake my head in awe. "And they say gymnastics isn't a brutal sport."

"I've had some bruises that would say otherwise. Although I've never seen my teammates punch each other in the face either. Maybe gymnastics is a more refined brutality than say, hockey."

I start to respond but then she grimaces. "Hang in there, baby."

"Almost done."

Dave, our tattoo artist, was supposed to close up shop an hour ago. He was kind enough to stay open for us when I offered to pay him double. Funny how that works.

He's worth it though. The work is good. Damn good. The swirls of blues and purples wrap around her ribs making a beautiful background for a script font that reads "More than Enough."

It's Ellery's ode to herself. A reminder that she's more than enough in the business world, in her personal world, and even for me.

"Okay, all done."

Dave wipes a few drops of blood off the area and helps Ellery up. "I'll cover it in a second but I figure you want to look first."

Ellery approaches the floor-length mirror and holds her shirt up as she moves from side to side. "It's exactly like I wanted," she breathes. "It's perfect."

"Just like you."

I don't mean to say that out loud, but it's true. Everything about Ellery is perfection. From the light in her eyes to the kindness in her actions. Even her new sense of style is exactly as she should be. Not for me, for her.

Dave strolls up with supplies in his hand, interrupts what somehow turned into an intimate moment. "You like it?"

Ellery nods excitedly. "I really do. Thank you so much."

"Yeah, no problem."

Dave begins slathering Ellery's rib with ointment and covering the new tat with some plastic to protect it while it heals. But I'm not paying attention to him. I'm too busy watching this beautiful woman as she takes in what she just did. When she looks up, we make eye contact and I feel a shift inside me.

Staring at each other in the reflection, I have a sudden sense of peace. A knowing that Ellery is my forever. I'm not sure if I love her yet. Those feelings take time and we haven't known each other long. But I'm getting there quickly and no matter what the future holds, I know Ellery is going to be part of it.

It's a huge revelation to be having inside a tattoo parlor and one I'm not ready to share yet. But someday I will. And I have a feeling that someday is coming soon.

NINETEEN
Ellery

It's a beautiful early October day, the sun and the humidity are low. My Halloween decorations are strung. It's the perfect day to go into the office late.

Or maybe it's my post-orgasmic bliss making everything seem more vibrant than it actually is.

I took half a day off, not because I had an appointment, but because after two months of complaining about being bored, Liam was finally cleared to work out again. He has to take it slow and still hasn't been given the okay to get back on the ice, which he wasn't happy about. But once those endorphins kicked into overdrive, Liam was like a starved man in all forms of physical activity. That includes any and all sexual positions he could find that didn't put too much strain on his shoulder.

Needless to say, I spent most of last night riding Liam good and hard. After that amount of exertion, I deserved to sleep in this morning.

I ride the elevator to the fourth floor, feeling confident in myself and the direction my life seems to be taking. I'm proudly wearing a new outfit Lauren helped me pick out on a recent shopping excursion, my hair is spiky almost in a faux hawk but very professional, and my tattoo is still vibrant under my shirt, reminding me of the secret ink no one in the building is privy to.

As I step off the elevator, my head held high, I wave at Brittany who is in the middle of a call. She's the only one I greet, because she's the only one not in the conference room. As I walk by the glass walls, it seems like the entire office is in there. I wonder if there is a meeting I didn't know about.

Dropping my purse in the drawer of my desk, I head back down the hall to see what's happening. I'd hate to miss something important. My clients deserve my best.

The mood in the conference room seems festive, but I'm not sure why. Everyone has a glass of what appears to be champagne in their hands. I suspect it's actually sparkling cider. Mrs. Welch would never go for publicly drinking in the middle of the day.

My co-worker Ruth quickly hands me a glass, just as Kevin's mom clinks her glass, indicating she's making a toast.

"If everyone would raise their glasses, please." The entire office complies, myself included, even though I have no idea what we're toasting. "To Kevin, my wonderful son. May you be as happy as I was with your father."

Wait… what is happening? I'm so confused.

Mrs. Welch continues. "And to Mallory. I've prayed for a woman like you to enter my son's life for years. I'm so glad you've finally arrived, and I can't wait to be your mother-in-law."

There's no way she just said what I think she said.

I lean to my right just slightly and sure enough, there

is Kevin with a huge smile on his face and his arm around a beautiful blonde who has a matching expression. They look at each other adoringly as they absorb Mrs. Welch's words.

My stomach drops along with the liquid out of the glass when my hand drops to my side. Ruth looks over at me, panic in her eyes. Just like everyone in the office, she knows Kevin and I were together for years. I know she's wondering if I'm about to make a scene. But I won't. I just hand her the empty glass, unconcerned with the mess I just made, and back out of the doorway slowly.

It's been two and a half months. Two and a half months since Kevin broke up with me. That's it. And he's already getting married?

I feel myself go numb as I hurry down the hall to my office and shut the door. My thoughts are swirling in a mixture of shock, outrage, disbelief, and indifference. It's overwhelming and I'm angry with myself that Kevin's sudden engagement stings as much as it does.

Don't cry, Ellery. Not here. Not in front of these people. Put on your mask. Pretend.

I suck back tears and try hard not to think about how Mrs. Welch just insulted me in front of the entire office. Everyone knows Kevin and I were dating. Everyone knows we broke up. I was passed up for a promotion and now she basically told everyone she never thought I was good enough for him anyway. Why would she do that? Did she never like me at all? Not even a little bit?

I race to my desk and open a file I've been working on trying to distract myself from the shock, but the numbers I see aren't computing. It's like my brain has completely shut down while every bad decision and insecurity I've ever had comes rushing back.

My opinions never counting. The apartment I was talked into renting. The job I turned down. And for what? I threw my life away on a man not knowing I was never what Kevin wanted. I was a placeholder until someone better came along.

I touch the area of my rib where the tattoo sits, trying to remind myself that I'm more than enough. That Kevin doesn't matter. And why should he? I'm happy with Liam. Liam who makes me smile and laugh and thinks I'm perfect the way I am. Liam is who I should be concentrating on. I wouldn't trade Liam for Kevin if I had the choice.

Still, this stings and I can't get the scene out of my head. *Mallory* is her name. The woman Kevin dumped me for. *Mallory* with long blonde hair and a tall, lithe body. She looks like a kindergarten teacher. We are nothing alike. Is that why he didn't want me?

Maybe even worse is the sudden insecurity I have about my new relationship. Will Liam find someone better suited for him, too? Will she have long blonde hair he can pull when they're in bed and he's doing her from behind? Will her makeup be subdued and glamourous? Will she dress in silks and satins and stare at him lovingly from under his arm as he holds her? Will she be smart and less neurotic? Will she be confident and less emotionally high maintenance?

I shake my head and blow out a breath. I have to get these irrational thoughts under control. I'm starting to spiral. I can do that later if I want. While I'm here, I will be the same hard-working employee I have always been, regardless of what anyone thinks. Mrs. Welch included.

I dab my eyes with a tissue to get rid of any moisture that shouldn't be there. Just in time for a knock on the door.

It's someone coming to check on me, I just know it.

I'm not in the mood to talk to anyone, but maybe if I pretend well enough, the office gossip will be how I'm completely over Kevin, not how hurt I am.

I take a deep breath and push all the conflicting feelings I have aside.

"Come in."

My voice is steady and my spine is straight. This is a good start.

Except it's Kevin walking through my door. That makes things harder. I want to kick him back out. To call him names and make him feel as bad as he's made me feel. But before I can get any words to come to me, he's sitting in the chair across from my desk.

Hold it together, Ellery. Do not let him see you hurting.

"I wanted to tell you myself."

I can feel one of my eyebrows raise. I don't even do it on purpose but the motion seems to have a strong effect on him. Suddenly he looks nervous.

"Then why didn't you?"

"I didn't have time. My mom started planning this engagement party a couple of weeks ago so she could throw it at a moment's notice. I guess I thought I'd have more than just a moment to tell you."

"You don't even work here Kevin."

He shrugs. "Family business, you know?"

I want to roll my eyes at how self-absorbed it all is. Instead, my head cocks to the side as I suddenly start to see the truth that they hid from me for longer than I realized. "She started planning weeks ago?"

"Yeah?" It's not a statement, it's a question. The more nervous Kevin gets, the more the pieces of a much larger puzzle start coming together.

"We broke up less than three months ago."

"Uh-huh." His cheeks begin to redden.

"And two months later, you were getting engaged."

"Okay?" He gulps. Loudly.

I'm not sure where my strength is coming from, but the longer this conversation continues, the more questions I want the answers to.

Clasping my hands together, I lean onto my desk. "I'm going to ask this once, Kevin, and if you respect me at all, I expect an honest answer. Were you cheating on me?"

"No!" he shouts then looks around as if there's someone else in here he shouldn't be disturbing with his outburst. "No. I knew Mallory from high school and we reconnected on social media a few months ago. But I promise we didn't start dating until after you and I broke up."

"Reconnected how?"

"What?"

I wave my hand around like he's an idiot for not understanding my question. At this point, it's either that, or he's trying to pull one over on me. I'm not sure which is the lesser of two evils.

"You said you reconnected on social media. How? Commenting on each other's posts? A group chat? Talking back and forth with just each other?"

He shifts in his seat as he tries to explain. "I don't know. I guess I reached out and we just started talking and catching up."

"Did you flirt?"

He puffs out a breath. "No. Of course not."

Somehow, I don't believe him. "Did she know you had a girlfriend at the time?"

"I don't know?"

"So you never typed the words, 'I have a girlfriend' in the months that you were talking?"

"I… it was so long ago, Ellery," he tries to argue. "I don't remember."

"Well, maybe you remember this." I lean back in my chair feeling quite confident that I finally have my answer to how our relationship went south so suddenly. "Did she send you pictures of herself? Selfies or nudes? And did you send any to her?"

He opens his mouth and closes it a few times, then wisely chooses to keep it shut. He may not consider what he was doing the definition of cheating, but he at least knows it was wrong.

"It all makes sense now," I mutter to myself. Kevin, of course, thinks I'm talking to him.

"What does?"

"You wanted her for a very long time. Had an emotional affair to try her on for size but kept me around in case things didn't work out with her. Then when your mother finally gave you the balls to ask her out, she said yes." His jaw drops with my crude word use, but I don't have it in me to care. "You waited until the last second to break up with me, just in case she changed her mind. And then you almost ran out of time, of moments, to be honest with me. That's why you did it so suddenly. You were out of time."

"It wasn't like that."

I hold up my hand to stop him. I'm tired of his excuses. "I'm pretty sure it was. In fact, I know it was. Because two months of dating before getting engaged isn't a very long time. Unless the other person involved thinks you've been together for much longer."

He shrugs and scratches the scruff on his cheek, trying hard to bow up and gain some control over the situation again. So, when the next words come out of his mouth, I'm not all that surprised. "When you know you know."

After seven years, he never knew with me. I shift in my seat, reminding me of my hidden mantra— a mantra that I am clinging to.

I am more than enough. Even if Kevin doesn't recognize it. Even if his mother doesn't see it at all. Even if I'm not feeling it in this moment, I am more than enough.

Straightening my back, I make a choice to be okay. Maybe I'll fall apart later, but for as long as I'm in the office, I will choose mind over matter. I will force myself to be the picture of perfectly fine. Even if I'm lying.

"Well. I'm glad to know you weren't *technically* cheating on me. And I'm happy you found a nice woman to date."

"Marry," he clarifies quickly probably knowing I said it on purpose.

"Yes. Sorry. To marry. I'm also dating so I suppose it makes things less awkward that we've both moved on."

"You're... dating?"

I bring Liam to the forefront of my mind, allowing thoughts of him to flood my brain. I almost feel guilty for using him to get in a dig at Kevin, but I can't stop myself. The look of shock on Kevin's face is so rewarding, I can't stop the smile that crosses my face.

"His name is Liam. I met him at..." I think twice about telling Kevin the name of the bar. It seems like a little hideout for Liam's team and I don't want to screw that up. "It doesn't matter where I met him. What matters is that he makes me happy."

Kevin's eyebrows raise ever so slightly, like he's unsure if I'm telling him the truth. "Really."

"Really. We have wonderful conversations, and we like some of the same things. He's a great cook. He even took me to a hibachi grill for our first date. I'm telling you, save up some money Kevin because it was so fun." I rest my chin on my fist allowing a content look to cross my face. "I never expected him to walk into my life, but here he is. And he has a cat."

Kevin's eyes narrow briefly, knowing I've always wanted a pet and he was the only reason I never acted on it. "And what does this guy think of your new hair?"

I'm taken aback at Kevin's blatant ugliness. Any lingering sadness and humiliation fade away as a new emotion takes over. Anger. Anger that I spent seven years on a man who was "unsure" of me. Anger that when I begin to learn who I truly am without regard for anyone else's opinions, it's still not enough. Anger that I was so easily discarded for a new, blonde model. And now that I know he's taken the gloves off, I'm ready for him to leave.

Narrowing my eyes, I clench my jaw tight. "What about my hair?"

"He likes it grey?"

"It's not grey, it's lavender. And I don't think he cares about the color. He likes it short, so he can nibble on the spot right here." I touch a spot toward the back of my neck that gives me goosebumps when Liam sucks on it. It reminds me that Kevin's opinion doesn't matter. Liam's doesn't either. But I sure do like that he likes it.

Kevin looks shocked, his mouth open but no words coming out. When there's another knock on the door, I'm grateful for the interruption. Until I see who it is.

"Is everything okay in here?" Mrs. Welch holds the door wide open, probably to make sure everyone within earshot can hear what's going on. Wouldn't want to miss Ellery breaking down, now would we?

Too bad for her I'm not a basket case right now. Not that anyone can see with her in the way anyway.

I flash her my brightest smile. "Yeah. Kevin was just saying hi."

"Oh." She looks surprised and almost disappointed by my nonchalant demeanor. "Well dear, you have a roomful of people who still want to congratulate you on your engagement so maybe the chit-chat can happen later?"

I don't miss the fact that she threw his pending marriage in there for my benefit. But also, there will be no later if I have anything to say about it.

"And I'm working on the Donnelly account so I really need to concentrate anyway," I say with another saccharine sweet smile.

"Right." Having been given his marching orders by two different people, Kevin stands up, looks at me, and whispers, "Right." Then he turns and walks out of my life. Hopefully for good this time.

She waits until Kevin is truly gone before eyeing me suspiciously. "Are Kevin's upcoming nuptials going to be a problem for you?"

"Of course not," I say quickly. "Like I was just telling him, I'm dating someone too so it's nice to see we've both moved on."

"Hmm." She doesn't sound convinced but I can't find it in me to care. I'm tired of her treatment. She's been beyond disrespectful lately, likely because she knows how sensitive I am and she loves having the upper hand. But no more. From now on, I have no interest in making nice with her. I'll be professional and do my job well, but that's all she'll get from me. No more, no less.

Realizing that's all I have to say, she finally turns tail and walks out, leaving me to stew.

At least I stew for a few minutes. The more I listen to the party down the hall, the one I'm not invited to and wouldn't go to even if I was, the more my bravado falls and the more disregarded I feel. It takes everything in me to make it through the day hoping I don't make any mistakes.

TWENTY
Liam

Pulling into the bar parking lot, I barely have time to put my truck into park because I'm out of it and racing to the front. Swinging the door open, Paul tilts his chin in greeting. I go straight to him to get the low down.

"Sorry for calling you, man. I cut her off already and Lauren's been trying to get her to go home with her but she refuses. Something about having the right to her opinions and right now her opinions say she needs to be at a bar."

I furrow my brow as I try and figure out what she's talking about. "That makes no sense."

"Nope. The only thing I've been able to decipher is that there is a man involved but I don't know in what capacity." His eyes narrow. "You didn't do anything to her, did you? I really don't feel like kicking your ass tonight."

While I appreciate Paul's protective nature over the women in his bar, it's unnecessary. "No. We left my place together this morning, well, closer to this afternoon, and things were fine. Great even."

Paul smirks in understanding. "I knew you were the right person to call. Kiersten told me things have gotten serious with you two lately."

"Obviously not as much as I thought if she's trying to get alcohol poisoning over some guy."

"Good point. Maybe I shouldn't have called you."

"No, it's fine. I'm glad you thought of me first, actually. I have a feeling I know exactly who this involves. Where is she anyway?"

I start to scan the room, trying to find the woman in question. Paul points to the other side of the bar where Ellery is looking drunker than the first night we met. Unfortunately, some of that sadness seems to be back as well. I suspect whatever happened took place at her job, which is why she's so shaken.

"Jaxon happened to swing by to talk to Kade about something so he's been hanging with her, keeping her out of trouble until you could get here."

"Appreciate it, man."

Paul nods and gets back to work filling an empty tray with drinks.

As I come around the bar, I realize Ellery doesn't even notice me. That's how hammered she is.

Coming up behind her, I wrap my arms around her waist. "I hear you're three sheets to the wind, sweets."

She spins around in my embrace, throwing her arms around my neck. "Liam! I'm so happy you're here! You like my hair right? And nibbling on this spot right here?"

She points to the spot on her neck that always gets her turned on.

I chuckle at how cute she is. "I do."

Leaning back in my arms, she stares right at Jaxon like he's offended her. "See? I told you."

"Yes, you did," he says with a nod and more nonchalance than most men would have under these circumstances. "Several times."

"Sorry," I mouth. He raises his beer to me, the universal sign of acceptance for my apology when a girlfriend gets drunk and obnoxious. "Hey sweets, I love this song. Why don't we go dance?"

I don't actually know what's playing, but if it gets her metabolism moving so she sobers up faster, she'll thank me in the morning.

She doesn't put up a fight, just follows me to the dance floor with a huge smile on her face.

Some fast-paced new hit is playing, but it's not smart for her to bounce around. Neither does seeing her vomit, nor seeing her face plant sounds appealing. So, I hold her close while we sway to our own music.

"Where's Lauren?"

Ellery throws her arm backward, waving it aimlessly. "She went to the bathroom. Or the office. Something. I don't know."

I hold back a smile. Drunk Ellery has always been entertaining Ellery. But something is bothering her and I want to know what.

"Wanna tell me what's on your mind?"

"Sure." She tries to waggle her eyebrows but it looks more like she has to sneeze. "I am thinking about you being naked and on top of me with your penis inside my vagina."

Her terrible attempt at dirty talk has me laughing out loud. "I think we're going to table that discussion for another night."

"You don't want me either." Her voice wobbles and I pull back enough to see tears stinging her eyes. The last time I saw her look like this was when that idiot broke up with her.

"Why wouldn't I want you? You're wonderful."

"No one does," she says sullenly. "I'm just a place-holder until someone else comes along."

I feel like I'm missing something significant.

"Is this about Kevin?"

"No." Her automatic defensiveness makes me know she's bullshitting me. "Kevin doesn't matter to me. I don't care about him or his new girlfriend who is blonde and beautiful and sent him nude pictures. They can get married all they want."

I think I'm starting to understand what's happening here. "Ellery, is Kevin getting married to someone else?"

She sighs deeply and drops her head on my chest. "Yeah."

If I was a better man, my concern would only be about her heartbreak. She loved Kevin for a lot of years, so it has to sting that he's moved on so quickly. But I'm not a better man and I feel a streak of jealousy run through me. Why is she dating me and hanging out at my house most nights if she's still hung up on him? And will she ever love me the way she loved Kevin?

For the most part, I feel pretty stable with this relation-ship, but now I'm starting to question Ellery's feelings for me. Even though I know there's still more to this story.

"Is that why you decided to come here and get drunk?"

It takes a few seconds for her to respond, and it occurs to me that she may have passed out and is only upright because I'm still holding her. I look down to see if her eyes are closed when she finally gives me an answer. "I don't want Kevin. I don't think I like him that much. Especially now that he cheated on me."

Suddenly it makes more sense. The boyfriend of so many years, the one she gave up a dream job for, the one who ran the show, was playing the field behind her back, only keeping her around until he found something better.

Jokes on him, though. No one is better than Ellery.

I kiss her on the top of the head and try to pull her closer. It's hard with our height difference. "You just found out he was cheating today?"

I feel her nod. "I found out everything today. They were having a giant staff meeting when I came in, telling everybody they were getting married because his mom had been praying for Mallory for years."

I don't know who Mallory is or why Kevin's mom was praying for her, but I can get the gist of what Ellery is saying. And I don't like the massive amount of disrespect that was thrown her way today.

I'm toying with leaving to go find that asshole and punch his face in for how fucking self-absorbed he is but Ellery starts talking more before I can move.

"Am I just a placeholder to you, Liam?"

My heart breaks as the root of the issue finally surfaces.

"No, baby. Not even close."

"I don't believe you," she slurs. "I don't even know if I'm the only girl you're having sex with. I never said I had to be your girlfriend first. Did I buy the milk and give away the cow for free?"

This time I don't bother stopping my chuckle. "I think it's the other way around."

"Around where?" She pulls away and begins looking over her shoulder. "Over there?"

"No, not that. Never mind." I pull her back to my chest, steadying her as she wobbles. "Just stay here and dance with me."

"Okay." She drops her head back on my chest.

"Ellery."

"Hmm." I don't think she even opens her eyes so I know I don't have long until she's done for the night.

"There is no one else in the world I want in my bed at night."

"Really? You mean me?"

"Really. And there's no one else I want to watch movies with or cook dinner with than you." I hug her tightly hoping she understands the gravity of what I'm saying. "And I already consider you my girlfriend even if I never said it."

"You do?"

"I do. And I'm sorry I made you feel like a placeholder."

She sucks in a deep, drunk breath. "You didn't. Kevin did. But he's a jerk face. And you're a... nice face."

"Oh well, that's very kind of you."

"If I'm your girlfriend, can I stay at your house tonight so you can big spoon me?"

"Absolutely. And if you're still awake for a while, I'll finish making the chicken pesto pasta I was working on before I came here."

"Ooh... chicken..."

Aaand we've officially moved onto the munchies portion of tonight's drunk fest.

I keep one arm around my newly official girlfriend so she doesn't fall down as we leave the dance floor and head back to the bar to close out her tab.

"You're such a good cook, Liam. You should start a YouTube channel for people who eat big meals. All those cooking shows have tiny little pieces of food. Who fills up on that? Do you have queso?"

179

I know what she just said was the result of a drunken rant, but it's like a lightbulb goes off in my brain.

I haven't been back on the ice yet and while that's the goal, retirement is probably coming in the next few years either way. What if I could make a living teaching other athletes how to cook?

"Huh," I say out loud as the idea rolls around in my brain a bit.

Turns out Drunk Ellery isn't just fun and entertaining, she's got some kick-ass ideas on how to make my future work, too.

Have to say, I didn't see that coming.

Just then she turns and pukes all over my shoes.

Didn't see that coming either.

TWENTY-ONE
Ellery

"Ohmygod I think I'm going to barf from all the cheese in this movie like Ellery barfs on shoes," Lauren complains making me blush. That was not my finest moment. "I don't care if she's an undercover reporter. You don't know that and you're a teacher. STOP FLIRTING WITH YOUR STUDENT, PE-DOPHILE!!" she yells at the big screen and shoves an-other spoonful of Rocky Road in her mouth.

"It was your idea to binge-watch a bunch of romantic comedies," Kiersten pops off and drops an almost empty pint of Chunky Monkey on the coffee table. She blows out a breath and sits back, rubbing her stomach. "I don't think it's the movie that's making me queasy. I think it's all the ice cream."

Annika sticks out her tongue in a gagging gesture and drops her ice cream on the table, too. "I can't eat this much dairy anymore. We're at the age now where I need a salad to offset all this sugar."

"Booo…" Lauren jeers. "You're all a bunch of lightweights. How are you doing over there, Ellery? Are you hanging with me or have you turned into a big baby like these two?"

I'm not sure how to answer her. I'm as nauseous as the others but I suspect mine is of the hangover kind and not sugar or movie related.

"To be honest, I could probably use more grease to balance out all the vodka from last night."

They laugh and Annika hands me almost all of her fried cheese sticks. She may have eaten half of one but that's all. Come to think of it, she hasn't drunk much at all today.

I was so embarrassed when I woke up this morning and realized I didn't just get drunk last night, I had a random emotional breakdown all over Lauren, Jaxon... Liam. And that was before I had all kinds of random vomit all over him, too. Word vomit and the regular kind.

Liam seemed completely unphased by the whole night, but I'm sure he thinks I'm a fruit loop now. I would. I'd prefer having no memory of blathering on about being Kevin's placeholder and putting Liam on the spot with his feelings. Unfortunately, I don't have that much luck. I guess purging my guts meant keeping my memories. Of all the nights to remember the things I said when I was drunk.

Liam swears he didn't take anything I said personally, but I don't know. I can't shake the feeling that I did some weird irreparable damage to our easy-going relationship.

Fortunately, I didn't have long to stew on it in front of him. Lauren showed up at his place with a large Irish coffee in hand for me calling it *hair of the dog*, and practically forced me into her car and to her place for what she called a mandatory girls' day.

So far all we've done is stuff junk food in our faces, sipped on mimosas, and critiqued a bunch of chick flicks.

And I've silently run through last night over and over in my brain.

"You were so toasted last night." I don't need the reminder from Lauren. It's all I can think about.

"Yeah, well it was a hard day."

I can't make eye contact, still embarrassed about my behavior. I keep my eyes trained on the screen and shove cold, fried cheese in my mouth, giving myself an excuse not to have to explain anymore.

Lauren doesn't take the bait, of course.

"Wanna tell us what Kevin did?"

No. I really don't. But considering she was one of the recipients of my hot mess last night, I feel like I owe her some kind of explanation.

I finally pull on my big girl panties and look at my oldest friend. She's normally tough as nails and doesn't care what anyone thinks of her. Right now, though, she has such a compassionate look on her face. This is the Lauren I know who has been through the emotional wringer herself and holds no judgment on anyone else because of it. Suddenly unloading my thoughts doesn't seem so bad.

"He didn't really do anything I guess. Just got engaged."

All three of my friends have various reactions of disbelief. None of them surprising. Not even Lauren's muttering that he's a donkey balls piece of shit.

"Hasn't he only been dating her for a couple of months?" I'm only slightly surprised Annika has been filled in on my life drama. These women have always been tight friends. It's part of why I like them.

"Supposedly they were friends in high school who reconnected online a few months ago." I shove another cheese stick in my mouth, hoping it shoves the sting of emotional pain down too.

Kiersten's eyebrows raise. "He had an emotional affair behind your back?"

I shrug, attempting at nonchalance but failing. "He swears nothing happened until we broke up."

"That's not how that works," Kiersten says. "I don't care if they didn't touch until three days ago. He's still a cheater. And none of that has to do with you. That's all about him and his small penis."

I wasn't expecting her to go there, so a much-needed laugh bursts out of me. I wouldn't call Kevin's penis small but compared to Liam, well, I suppose they're both proportional to their body types and Kevin was a competitive gymnast. They're not known for being large.

"Don't you work for his mom?" Annika asks. I haven't seen her at Frui Vita since this whole crappy situation began so I'm not surprised she has a few questions for me. "How is that going now that you guys aren't together?"

I huff out a breath. "Well, I've been passed over for a promotion I was promised without even being interviewed, and I walked into an engagement party yesterday where my boss announced to my entire office she was so glad Kevin finally found someone worthy of the Welch family name."

"Oh, fuck that shit," Lauren blurts out. "Kevin has always been a follower and I guarantee his mom picked this bitch out for him because she can push them both around. You're so much better than that."

"I know." I don't really know. At least I don't feel like it yet. But I'm hoping the more times I say it the sooner I'll believe it.

"You need a new job," Annika remarks and takes a sip of her water even though she has a full mimosa sitting right in front of her. Is that still the first one from three hours ago?

"She's right," Kiersten says with a nod. "You're in accounting, right? Have you put out any feelers yet?"

"I have." I feel my face begin to blush. "Actually, Liam tipped me off to an opening in his team's corporate office."

"What?" Lauren's face lights up and she bounces lightly on the couch. "Did you send it?"

"A few weeks ago. I haven't heard anything back though."

"That's totally normal," Kiersten says. "Paul has only had to hire people at the bar a couple of times, but when he does it takes forever. He has to post about it, then gather resumes and sort through them. And he has to keep doing all the other stuff to keep the bar running at the same time. It takes a while for him to get through it all."

Annika gives her a quizzical look. "Hasn't he only hired friends and family lately?"

"Why do you think that is?" Kiersten replies. "It's a pain in the ass trying to find the right person from an employment website. Word of mouth works best for us. Maybe word of mouth will work for you too, Ellery."

I'd prefer my skills to hold up on their own without Liam's help, but I keep that to myself. She's just trying to be supportive and I appreciate it.

"Forget the job tip." Lauren holds up her hand like she has something much more important to discuss. "I need to know what's going on with you and that hot hockey player. You've been spending an awful lot of nights with him for what, a couple of months? Please tell me he's amazing in the sack and scratching the itch Kevin could never reach."

Kiersten groans and Annika throws a pillow at Lauren's face. She just grabs it and plops it on her lap.

"Oh yeah. Pretend like you two don't want to know all the dirty details."

I pull the plate closer to my face and take another bite. I'm not really hungry, just using it to hide behind. Lauren purses her lips at me and pulls the plate down onto my lap.

"Fine. I don't need dirty. But at least tell me what's going on. Is it serious?"

It feels weird to share my innermost thoughts about Liam with them. I know what he said last night, but I'm not totally positive he wasn't trying to pacify me in my time of need. What if I like him more than he likes me? I'll feel humiliated if any of them say they've seen him flirt with other women or something. But I'm tired of trying to figure it out on my own and they're here, being supportive after an unusually difficult evening. Maybe sharing a little piece of my soul with them will help me figure things out and even bring me some closer friendships. Or maybe it'll backfire on me. I guess at this point I don't have anything to lose.

"Maybe?"

Lauren gives me the same look my mother does when she's disappointed in me. "Nu-uh. That's a cop-out. What are you really feeling?"

I rub my forehead and squeeze my eyes shut. Why is it so hard to talk about feelings? Actually, I know why. I'm afraid of being crushed. It seems easier to hold my feelings close to my chest than trust anyone else with them. I really need to stop that.

"I admit I like him. *Really* like him. But don't you think it's too soon? I met him like two hours after Kevin broke up with me."

"So what?"

"So, I'm afraid he's a rebound for me." I look down at

my hands and fidget with my nails. "And I'm afraid I'm just a stand-in for him until he finds someone better."

Lauren laughs lightly. "I saw the look on his face when you boohooed all over him last night. That man's heart was breaking because you were in pain. And what did he do? Pulled you tighter and kissed you on top of the head."

He did? I don't recall that part.

Kiersten nods vigorously. "I wasn't there last night but I've seen the way he looks at you, with googly eyes and shit."

Lauren rears back. "He does, doesn't he?" Kiersten smiles and nods again.

"I know you think they're biased," Annika adds. "But when Jaxon got home, he said the same thing, and guys don't notice stuff like that."

I cock my head. "Notice what? What did he say?"

"He was laughing that Liam was the latest victim of the love bug. That's what he called it."

Kiersten covers her heart and says, "Awww," while Lauren cackles.

"He's got a love bug. That's awesome. Way better than crabs."

I ignore Lauren's joke because it really does help hearing their take on things. But I still can't shake the anxiety I feel over all of this.

"You really think he's serious about me?"

Lauren grabs my hand and squeezes. "I do. And I'm pretty pissed that Kevin did such a number on you that you have to even question true love when you see it."

I furrow my brow, laughing lightly. "True love, that's a stretch."

All three of them shake their heads.

Love. Huh. I hadn't allowed myself to think that intensely, but I could love Liam. Someday, anyway. He'd be wonderful to be in love with.

As those thoughts take root, I begin to feel a little better. Maybe Kevin was a way worse boyfriend than I gave him credit for. But that doesn't mean I should compare Liam to him. They're not the same person. Not at all. If I ever got drunk with Kevin, he would have reprimanded me for it regularly, after telling his mom, of course. And I don't even want to know how he'd react if I puked on his shoes. But Liam, he just seems to adjust to any situation, good or bad, and likes me anyway.

Feeling some relief and having a different perspective, I'm ready to move on to a lighter topic. But first, I need more ice cream.

I hand the remaining cheese sticks over to Annika. "You want these back? I'm in the mood for something sweeter."

She grimaces, as if just looking at them makes her sick. "Please. No. Keep them far away from me before I hurl."

"What is the matter with you lately?" Lauren asks. "You're eating like a bird and you haven't even taken a sip of your drink. I even used the good champagne. You're not on some stupid diet, are you?"

Annika shoots Lauren a look like she's lost her mind. But Kiersten's jaw is the one that drops.

"No. Way."

Annika looks at Kiersten and some sort of telepathy seems to exchange between them before Annika crinkles her face and nods. And that's when Kiersten screams.

"Motherfucker," Lauren yells, and pushes on her ear. "Can you scream any louder in my ear?"

Kiersten isn't listening, though. She's climbing over legs and tables and food to get to Annika where she hugs her tight, still squealing.

"When did you find out? How far along are you? Ohmygod, our babies are going to grow up together!"

And that's when the lightbulb clicks for Lauren who screams so loudly, I'm pushing on my ear now.

"Ohmygod you're pregnant!!!" Lauren gets down on the floor to crawl over to her friend and starts talking to Annika's stomach while the mom-to-be laughs. "Hi, baby. I'm your Auntie Lauren. Your Uncle Heath is the best uncle in the whole world so I can't wait for you to come over and play."

"I thought Jaxon couldn't have kids," Kiersten says, practically sitting on my lap as she keeps close to the almost new mom. "How did this happen?"

"We didn't know if he could have them." Annika leans around Kiersten so she can see me. "He had cancer as a kid so it's one of those things where you don't know until you try."

"You've been trying?" Lauren asks as she rubs Annika's nonexistent baby bump. Watching this whole scene unfold is pretty humorous.

"More like, we haven't been *not* trying."

"But you feel good about this? About the baby and working and everything?"

Annika bobs her head. "I'm scared. And I have no idea how I'm supposed to be a trainer for a sports team if I'm carrying around a basketball in my shirt. But I guess I'll figure it out eventually."

Lauren sighs and leans in for another hug. Almost immediately, Kiersten goes in for her own squeeze and drags me in with her until the four of us are a pile of hugging limbs.

I may still be mad at Kevin and that hurt might linger

for a while, but breaking up with me was the best thing he's ever done for me. It led me to that bar where I reconnected with women who have become my biggest supporters and really great friends.

There's no better gift than that.

TWENTY-TWO
Liam

One of the worst parts of being injured is all the damn paperwork that has to be filled out.

I may have a contract and get paid a lump sum, but there are still forms that have to be read over and signed: liability, disability, insurance. Most of it is a legal formality to cover the organization's butt, but it still requires my John Hancock, which is the only reason I'm showing my ugly mug in the corporate offices today.

I'd rather be at home napping. My body is wiped. I finally got clearance to get back on the ice, but only to start with basic drills. Absolutely no body-checks or contact of any kind. I'm itching to get back to it, but I have to admit it was nice to at least be on my skates this morning, doing some sprints, shooting some pucks, and getting my body back into the motion that I love.

There's another kind of motion that I love but I'll have to wait for that until Ellery gets off work tonight. That woman is under my skin and I don't hate it. I love hanging out with her, even when she's having an emotional moment.

The fact that she trusts me with her vulnerability is a huge turn-on. It's like she knows I'm different than the others. Or "other" in her case. And that she knows on a subconscious level that I'm the one for her. I'm the yin to her yang. It makes me eager to skip through the dating part and get to the forever.

I huff a laugh at myself. I never expected me, Liam Trembley, San Antonio Slingers hockey player with my sport as my one true love to fall for someone else. But I did. There's no use denying it to myself. I'm in love with Ellery McIlroy with her purple hair and slightly neurotic thoughts. I love her even more than I love hockey.

Never saw that coming.

My mom is going to freak out when I finally admit it to her. But Ellery deserves to know first, and she's not ready yet. Close, but not quite.

The elevator dings as I reach the floor for human resources so I refocus my attention on getting in and out as fast as possible. The longer I'm here, the hungrier I get and I've been dying to try cooking a braised chicken. My mouth waters just thinking about it. Once that sucker gets in the oven, I'll have a solid half an hour to nap on the couch. Or maybe I should try making a video of me cooking it.

I scoff and push that thought right out of my mind. Ellery's intentions were good when she suggested it but the ramblings of a broken-hearted drunk don't always make the best ideas.

I weave my way through the large room heading toward the back. Seeing players around the office isn't unusual for the administrative staff, but I still get a few double-takes as I make my way around the maze of desks. They better get used to it. If Ellery gets the accounting job, I'll be spending more time up in this area. Even if it's just to take her to lunch every day if she can get away. The idea of us working so close together makes me feel giddy.

I rap my knuckles on the door jamb of the HR office.

The middle-aged redhead looks up from her desk, flashing me a smile and waving me in. "Liam! Hey there. Come on in."

Annie Hughes has been the head of HR for as long as I've been here. Probably longer. She's always been easy to talk to and made the transition from active player to injured list so much easier to bear. Honestly, I'm not sure I would have made it through the disappointment of surgery without her honest, but compassionate attitude.

"I hear you have clearance to be on the ice again. How'd it feel?"

Unlike a lot of people who work behind the scenes, Annie is a true hockey fan but is never a fangirl. She's always interested in how practices are going and what our thoughts are on the competition. I'm not sure if she's always been that way or if she decided there are job perks if she enjoys hockey when she started working here. Regardless, it's fun shooting the shit with her.

"I'm going to be sore tomorrow, that's for sure." I smile. No amount of Icy Hot will ruin the feeling I have knowing I can be back on the ice. "But it's worth it."

"Still have restrictions though, right? Wearing the no-contact jersey like you're supposed to?"

"Yes, ma'am. Doc said I'm almost ready but wants to give me a couple more weeks before going at full throttle again. You know how he is about body-checks anyway."

She flashes me a look and begins sorting through some papers on her desk. "Every time one of you goes down,

I get an earful from him about the long-term dangers of playing professional hockey."

I laugh. "Does he think you can change the rules of the game or is he just hoping every player in the league will come to their senses and quit?"

"You got me. He's a great doctor but between you and me, I think he just wants to make sure I know how important he is." She continues to shuffle things around, beginning to look flustered. "Sorry I don't have the paperwork right here ready for you. Do you know what a pain it is to find a new payroll manager?"

"Is that the position you have open? I thought it was accounting?" Maybe this is why Ellery hasn't heard from them yet.

"It is. Payroll is under the accounting umbrella, it's just such a big job it's the only thing that person does." Grabbing one pile of papers, she drops them at the front of her desk where I can see them better. "This is my stack of good candidates. I've already sorted through the 'thank you, no thank yous'. Now I need to figure out who I should call first. It's such a nightmare trying to go through these and do my job and try to help with payroll."

"Wait, you don't have anyone doing payroll right now?"

Annie stops what she's doing and holds her hands up. If hand gestures are involved, she's going into full-on story mode. "She quit. Didn't put in her two weeks' notice. Just quit. Walked in a few weeks ago and said she was going to Tahiti or something to find her Zen. Which is great. More power to her. But by God, give me two weeks' notice before you do so I can get some things set in place before you go. It really put us in a bind. Especially with the last of the contract revisions and trades happening." She shakes her head. "I swear the first person I see in that stack who can do the job and do it well is hired. I'm so annoyed by the whole thing." Annie shakes her head. "It also means my brain is spinning which is why I can't find what I'm looking for."

"Don't worry about me. It's not going to hurt my feelings if it takes a few extra minutes to find my paperwork. Would it be easier if I come back tomorrow?"

Annie pushes her chair back and away from her desk. "Actually no. My boss is already breathing down my neck to get this done so he can stop paying into your disability."

I snicker. That sounds like the GM.

"I just realized I asked Marissa to hold your paperwork for me so I didn't lose it in this pile. Hang on." Annie darts out of the room shouting to someone on the other side of the office about my file.

I can see why she's irritated. It looks like a paper bomb went off in her office. On her desk in particular. I wish there was something I could do to help her out. She's a nice lady. She deserves a break.

Glancing at the pile of resumes, my eye snags on one sticking out from the middle. The only part showing says "Ell". I know who that belongs to. And I know what I need to do with it.

I look behind me to make sure the coast is clear, even though I'm not doing anything wrong. I'd still be embarrassed if I was caught, just trying to explain I'm not going through Annie's stuff. The last thing I need is for this to be some sort of privacy violation I don't know about. But I know who she needs and if I can help Annie find her quicker, what's the harm in that?

Quickly, I pull Ellery's resume out from the middle of the pile and put it right on top. If she has the skills Annie is looking for, she'll get a call. And boy does she need the chance to get out of the dead-end job she's working at now. A change of environment could go a long way in helping her heal from her hurts.

I'm already lounging back in my chair, phone in hand, reading over the recipe I'm going to try when Annie finally makes it back.

"Sorry that took so long. Marissa's desk looks a lot like mine these days. I swear we're normally more organized than this."

"It's fine." I take the pen she offers and begin signing my name next to all the little flag stickers as she presents them to me. "I just hope you find who you're looking for in that pile. Fingers crossed they'll be right near the top for you."

"You have no idea how badly I want that."

Actually, I do. I may want it more than she does.

Annie flips the page. "And one more right here and... then... you're... done."

Handing it back to her, I blow out a relieved breath. I'm so glad to have my job back. I guess I never lost it, but it still feels better to be back on a regular roster.

Standing up, I shove my phone in my pocket. "Thank you for making that relatively painless."

She walks to a filing cabinet and pulls the third drawer open, fingering through some files before putting mine where it goes. "I'd say something standard like 'hope it doesn't take as long next time to see you again' but I'm not sure either of us wants a next time."

"If it means me being injured again, I'd rather not see you for a while."

We both laugh at my quip.

"Anyway, good luck with your candidate search."

"Thanks," she calls and I can already tell she's back in work mode just by how her eyes zero in on something on her desk, probably whatever she needs to finish.

And I thought my job was hard. I'll take being rammed into a wall and blisters on my feet any day of the week if it keeps me away from working in this office. The only time I hope to come back here is when I take my girlfriend to lunch. Fingers crossed a strategically placed resume will help me do just that.

TWENTY-THREE
Ellery

I can't believe I got the call.

When Liam told me about the job at the Slinger's corporate office, I didn't think it would ever amount to anything. Of course, I sent my resume because I wasn't going to totally dismiss it. But it never crossed my mind that I'd get an actual interview.

But I did. And here I am. Riding the elevator to the fourth floor so I can meet the HR manager who will decide if she thinks I'm a good fit.

Just knowing she'll be assessing me from the second I step out of this lift has my nerves on edge. I don't remember being this anxious when I interviewed for my current job. Then again, I don't remember it being a real interview either. It was more a formality to make sure the rest of the staff didn't immediately assume there was some weird semi-nepotism thing happening.

In hindsight, I'm positive there was. Welch and Associates is a family-owned business. If Mrs. Welch assumed I was going to marry Kevin eventually, she was probably grooming me to run the business upon her retirement.

Well, she *was*. Until she decided there was a better candidate for daughter-in-law.

I won't think about that now. I have a new person to wow with my abilities and even if I don't get the job, every interview is good practice for the next one.

Smoothing my black pencil skirt down and ensuring my billowy white blouse is still buttoned properly, I blow out a breath just in time for the elevator doors to part.

The office is wide open—no closed in rooms or cubicles. Just open desks so people can interact while they work. I like that.

The sound of the chatter gives the room a different vibe. Glancing around, I notice mostly women working here—only one man. As people catch my eye, I get smiles in greeting.

Wow. What a different feeling than at my current job where everyone keeps to themselves and any interruptions are treated with irritation. I wonder what it would be like to work in an environment like this one.

Approaching the first desk I see, I'm greeted with yet another smile. I can't tell how old the man is, although once people are over twenty-five, I have a hard time being able to tell anymore. His black-rimmed glasses make him look intelligent, but not pompous. I like his vibe immediately.

"Good morning," he says with a comforting smile as he rips up a piece of paper and tosses it in the garbage. "What can I do for you today?"

"I have an interview with Annie Hughes and I'm not sure where to go. I'm Ellery McIlroy."

"Oh, of course." He hops out of his chair, I mean literally hops, and waves for me to follow him. "I'm Jared and we're so glad you're here. Things have been a little tense without this position filled."

This is tense? Everyone seems so happy to be working here. It makes me wonder what it would be like when there isn't an open position.

People continue to smile at me while we wander around a bunch of desks.

"Wow. Everyone seems so nice, though."

"You're coming from an accounting firm, right?"

I nod, not quite sure what that has to do with anything.

"I used to work for a firm, too. The vibe here is nothing like that rat race. It's much more of a family feel here. We have a job to do and we need to do it right, but I will never go back to that kind of office again if I can help it."

"That's some high praise."

"It helps that Annie is such a great boss. Speaking of which…"

We stop in front of an office door I didn't notice before. Jared knocks on the door jamb and leans into the office. "Knock, knock. Ellery is here."

I can't see who he's talking to but I hear a female voice respond with "Oh good!"

Jared backs out of the doorway. "Annie, this is Ellery. Ellery, our fabulous boss Annie."

The woman in question is easily in her fifties with curly, bright red hair pulled back with a clip. Her easy smile has my nerves immediately tapering off as she puts her hand out for me to shake.

"It's so nice to meet you. Come on in and have a seat. Thanks, Jared," she calls to him as he retreats back to his workspace. "I need to apologize for the mess in here. I'm hoping things get back to some sort of normalcy once we get this position filled."

"Jared was telling me it's a bit crazy right now."

She huffs a laugh as we both sit. "Let's just say I'm so glad your resume was on the top of my pile and you were able to come in so quickly. I'm ready to pass payroll work back to someone else."

She settles in her seat and puts some reading glasses on, then glances over my resume.

"Are you a hockey fan, Ellery?" Annie asks without looking up from the paper.

"I hate to admit this but not really."

She looks up, her eyebrows raised just slightly. "Have you ever been to a game?"

I shake my head. "I know a couple of the team members through some mutual friends." Mutual friends being a bar we all frequent, and a bed that I slept in last night. She doesn't need to know that part, though. "But team sports aren't something I naturally gravitate toward."

She pauses for a few seconds, assessing me. It makes me nervous again so words begin pouring out of my mouth.

"Not that I couldn't learn to have team spirit, of course. On game days or whatever events we would need to go to. I can buy a spirit shirt…"

My words taper off as she smirks, seeming amused by my word vomit.

Picking up my resume, she ignores my nervous chatter and glances at the short list of my career accomplishments again. "I see you've been a junior accountant for Welch and Associates for the last few years. How many accounts do you oversee?"

"About twenty, give or take depending on the month."

"Is that mostly payroll?"

"Payroll, taxes, some accounts requisitions. Basically, anything money-related that the company needs me to do."

"So, a jack of all trades." Annie leans back in her chair and tosses her glasses on her desk. "What we need is someone who can focus on payroll."

My heart sinks a little. While I can do payroll, it feels like a step down from what my goals have been. I was on track to be a senior accountant, in charge of margins and expenditures for some good-sized corporations. Still, I'm here in a very different kind of environment and I'm curious what Annie has to say.

"The title of Payroll Manager sounds a little deceiving," she continues. "Because of the kind of business we're in, payroll means something different for almost every employee. We have hourly, salary, lump sums, bonuses. And that's just the people under the Slingers umbrella. We also have international employees and contractors who require a whole different kind of payout. Nothing is cut and dry and paydays aren't just locked into one or two particular days a month."

The more she explains what the job really is, the more interested I become. This isn't just cutting checks every two weeks. This is part of managing an entire organization's money. And this organization is larger than anything I would ever work with at my current job. There's no way I could get bored here. And in an environment like this, it could be more of my dream job than a senior accountant ever was.

Or maybe my dreams are just changing. And maybe that's okay too.

"I'm sorry I'm rambling," Annie says with a small smile. "I want to make sure the job responsibilities are on the table. It's not just about whether or not we want you. It's about whether you want us, too. Do you have any questions for me?"

Her words make me feel warm inside. I recognize how odd my reaction is, but for so many years I've just been a cog in a wheel that doesn't care about their employees as much as I thought. To work in a place that truly thinks their employees are family is exciting.

"Are there any kind of advancement opportunities?"

"Yes and no. Obviously, there are a limited number of positions in this particular office, but this isn't our owner's only venture. He owns quite a few businesses that are always expanding and growing. So, if you ever feel stifled here and don't want to move into managing benefits, working for him somewhere else is always a possibility as well. Speaking of which, I'm sure you're curious about salary and benefits."

"I wasn't going to say anything at this point, but it's something that I've wondered about."

When she tells me the number, my jaw drops open in shock. I knew the players were well compensated but I had no idea the administration was also rewarded so handsomely.

"Yeah, that's the same reaction I had when I first started working here," Annie admits. "And if you think that's good, just wait until you see the benefits package. So let me ask you a question. Why are you trying to leave your current job?"

I've always been the girl who doesn't quite know what to say in sticky situations. Do I tell the truth? Do I fudge things a little? What is the best course of action that won't hurt me but isn't just a bold-faced lie? I'm never sure I'm making the right choice. This situation is no different.

How do I tell the woman I'm hoping will become my new boss that my old boss threw my life into a complete upheaval and has created a very difficult work situation?

It's not a hostile environment, per se, but it's not ideal either.

Still, I don't want to come across as a potential problem employee so I opt to not say too much.

"I thought I wanted to work in an accounting firm and work my way up the ladder."

"And that's changed?"

I stop to think because, after the short time I've been in this interview, I can definitely feel some different aspirations growing inside me.

Carefully, I choose my next words. "I'm beginning to think opportunities arise in places we don't always expect. And I think I'd rather have a great work-life balance while I keep my eyes open for those opportunities, than always be scrambling to prove my worth. I can be a hard worker and a strong asset to a team and still work in an environment that values me as a person, not just an employee number."

I watch as Annie's eyes narrow. I'm not sure if she's assessing me again or thinking, but soon enough a smile crosses her face.

"That may be one of the best answers I've ever gotten to that question."

Sighing with relief, I can't stop my own grin. I like Annie. I like this office. And I'm almost positive I could like this job. I just have to get it.

"So." Annie folds her hands and leans forward on her desk. "What other questions can I answer for you?"

TWENTY-FOUR

Liam

"It was amazing, Liam."

Ellery's excited voice comes through the speaker loud and clear. She's been chattering for several minutes and I'm not complaining. For someone who normally worries if she's saying too much, I appreciate this new comfort level with me. But since there are no signs she'll stop any time soon, I finally put her on speakerphone so I can keep peeling these zucchinis to make "noodles". I'm not sure if I'll like them yet, but it's worth a shot.

"Have you met Annie before?"

"I have," I say with a nod she can't see. "Talked to her last week when I signed all that disability paperwork."

"She's amazing," Ellery gushes. "I feel like I could learn so much from her about how to manage people and an office. I'm in your driveway, by the way."

I hear her car door slam through my phone and out front at the same time. "Door is open. I'm in the kitchen."

"Seriously, Liam. I think I want to be her when I grow

up. I mean I don't want to do HR necessarily but maybe spearhead one of the departments, not just payroll."

The front door closes and I can still hear her talking a mile a minute as she walks down the hall. It's like she's in stereo. I don't mind. The fact that she's so excited she doesn't want me to miss a word she says makes me happy for her.

"The salary is more than I expected and the benefits package…" Ellery walks into the room and disconnects her phone but keeps talking. "…I had no idea the Slingers organization provides so well for their employees."

She approaches without hesitation and follows the instructions printed on my apron and gives the cook a quick kiss.

"Hi."

"Hi."

"Sorry I'm babbling."

"Don't be sorry. I like hearing you so excited."

She kisses me again then uses her thumb to wipe some lipstick off my lips. "I had to go to my actual job after the most amazing interview. Do you know how hard it was to stay focused and not want to tell everyone about it? It's been trying to bubble out of me all day." She glances around my counter. "What are you making, anyway?"

"Currently, zucchini noodles. But I'm trying to pair it with a twist on chicken parm."

"Sounds good."

"We'll see. I'm not liking the look of these zoodles so far."

"Zoodles?" she asks with a laugh.

I shrug. "I have no idea if that's a real thing but it sounds good so I'm running with it." I gesture to the glass of water I have waiting for her on the large island. "Have a seat."

She makes herself comfortable on one of the stools and takes a long drink. Ellery may switch to wine or something later, but I've learned she prefers a large glass of water when she gets home from work. I wouldn't be surprised if she forgets to hydrate during the day, getting too engrossed in her work. I should get her one of those giant water bottles that mark off what time you should have certain amounts consumed. She'd probably get a kick out of it.

"So did Annie offer you the job yet?"

"No. And I'm trying not to get too excited. I'm not the only person she's going to interview. It was just so eye-opening to see a different way of doing my job. That I don't have to work in a place that doesn't care about me as a person. It feels like there are so few places like that anymore."

Finishing off one zucchini, I eye my future zoodles skeptically. I know they aren't going to look like regular pasta but the color and shape are throwing me off.

"What?" Ellery asks.

"I'm just trying to figure out how these things aren't going to fall apart when I boil them."

"Have you never made these before?"

"Nope. And suddenly it seems like a bad idea."

Ellery smiles with amusement. "You've already gotten this far. You may as well keep going with them. If they turn out terrible, you know not to bother doing them again."

She's got a point. Picking up my peeler and the largest zucchini of the bunch, I get back to work. I'm sure she's hungry after the day she's had and I'm ready to feed her.

"What did you think of the office anyway? Is it as chaotic as it was last week?"

"I don't really have a reference point, but it didn't seem

that bad. Now that you mention it, though, they were really happy to see me."

That causes me to laugh. "I'm not surprised. Annie's office was a mess when I was there and that's not like her at all. She showed me her stack of resumes and mentioned the first person in the pile who meets her qualifications was basically hired."

A strange look crosses Ellery's face, one that I can't quite decipher. "And mine happened to be the first one?"

"It was in the middle but when she walked out of the room I happened to see it so I put it on top. I knew she'd love you."

"Wait." Ellery holds her hand up, her demeanor completely changing. "You put my resume on the top of the pile?"

It's at this moment that I realize I've made a huge mistake. My happy, chatty girlfriend who was excited about a new opportunity just flipped personalities and looks like I kicked her puppy. I'm not sure if my error was moving her resume or telling her about it, but either way, I know I've screwed up royally.

"Why would you do that, Liam?"

"I… I didn't know it was wrong. Annie was stressed and having a hard time finding a good candidate. I knew you were a good candidate. It seemed like a way to help you both."

Ellery stands up, hands on her hips. Her legs are planted wide and her whole body is tense. I'm not sure I've ever seen her this mad. Oddly, it makes me happy to see her showing intense emotions like this and standing up for herself, even if I'm still not quite sure what I did wrong.

"You realize my last boyfriend got me a job too and look where I'm at now."

And now I'm slightly offended. "What the hell does that dick have to do with me?"

She throws her hands up in the air in frustration. "The minute that relationship went south, it's become a nightmare to go into work. I'm the laughing stock of the whole office. And let's not forget the promotion I was passed over for. I don't want that to happen again, Liam."

Now I understand. This isn't so much about what I did. It's about her fear of what could eventually happen. I hate that she still doesn't trust my intentions and that even if our relationship did end, she's still afraid my integrity is only short-lived. Even worse, I hate that she thinks there's an expiration date on what we have.

"I'm not even going to comment about the fact that you're already planning on us calling it quits." Putting the zucchini down, I wipe my hands on a towel and round the island. "That stings, but it doesn't change the fact that I'm also sorry, Ellery. I never thought of it that way. I promise I never spoke your name. Annie has no idea we know each other or that we're dating. All I did was put one piece of paper on top of the stack so she'd see it first. Her phone call to you, the interview, that was based on your accomplishments, not anything I did."

"It doesn't matter Liam. Don't you see?" she pleads. I hate seeing that look in her eyes. "I can't go to another job because my boyfriend got me in. I can't have you assuming I need your help. I have to be able to do this on my own, otherwise…"

Her words taper off and her eyes get misty.

"Otherwise, what?" I whisper.

She looks away and takes a deep, steadying breath. "Otherwise, I'll never know I can stand on my own two feet."

"Ellery…" I take a step forward and reach to her, hoping to convince her that she's one of the strongest people I know. But she steps back, out of my reach.

"No. I'm serious. I can't be this weak pushover anymore. I need to be able to do this on my own —get my own jobs and pick my own apartment. I've let other people's opinions influence my life for way too long. I can't do that again."

My heart starts pounding at the implication of her words.

"What does that mean for us?"

"I don't know."

I take a step back, wiping my mouth with my hand, shock running through me. Seconds ago, we were discussing noodles made out of a vegetable and now she's questioning our whole relationship?

"Are you breaking up with me? Over this?"

I have to clarify with her that this is just a misunderstanding. That she needs time to lick her wounds but that we'll be fine in the end and that she knows it too.

Instead, she gives me nothing to make me feel better.

"I don't know." Ellery crosses her arms over her chest and looks at the floor. This woman I've fallen in love with, the feisty, naïve, inquisitive woman I can't get enough of may already want to call it quits.

The air is knocked right out of me. This is the worst thing that could happen. It's worse than when I burned the braised chicken the other day. It's worse than when Tucker gave my phone number out to a legitimately disturbed puck bunny who called four hundred eighty-seven times in two days. It's worse than when I found out I was having surgery and was benched for twelve weeks.

My legs almost give out, but my butt finds the stool she

was just sitting on first.

"What can I do to fix this?"

She shrugs and I know in this moment, it's all on her. There's nothing I can do to make this right. Nothing I can say to ease her concerns. Ellery needs to think through the situation and decide if she trusts me enough to know I would never intentionally or even flippantly harm her. And while my actions speak louder than my words, her wounds are deeper than my love.

"I just need some time."

Closing my eyes, I hold back the moisture that wants to build. Getting teary over giving her time won't do either of us any good. She's spooked. She needs to assess the danger level on her own. And I have to let her. I have to trust in us enough to know she'll find the truth through all her fear.

When I'm finally feeling solid again, I open my eyes and just look at her. When she finally catches my gaze, I give her what she needs. An out.

"Take whatever time you need. I'll be here waiting for you."

She nods once, grabs her stuff, and leaves quietly. The snick of the door closing reverberates like she slammed it right through my heart.

TWENTY-FIVE
Ellery

Concentrating on work has been the only thing keeping me sane lately. Ever since I stormed out of Liam's house, pissed that he gave me a leg up on the job applicant competition, I've been questioning myself and why I'm so mad. I haven't come up with any answers yet, but I sure have been keeping it locked up in a nice tight little box in my brain.

I've been so hyper-focused that when my office phone rings, I jump. Calls are never transferred to me. My clients all have my cell if they need to reach me and if they call the front, usually it's something the office staff can handle anyway. I almost forgot the phone has a purpose beyond being a paperweight.

I shuffle a few things around and pull it closer to me before picking up the receiver.

"This is Ellery."

"Hi, Ellery. It's Annie Hughes from the San Antonio Slingers. How are you?"

My heart leaps and plummets at the same time. I'm

excited to hear from her, but it's also yet another reminder that I haven't talked to Liam in two days.

I feel bad for walking out on him the way I did. I know he only had good intentions when he made sure my resume was on the top of the pile. But I can't shake the feeling it gives me that he thinks I'm inept. And that everyone else will too if I were to take the job. Plus, what the fallout would look like if we were to break up. It just feels icky to me.

Logically, I know that's mostly just my own insecurities, but I can't shake them. The longer I go without contacting Liam though, the worse I feel when I do allow that little box to crack open. Annie's phone call isn't just a reminder that I need to get my act together, it's also keeping me from distracting myself with the numbers. I've been way more productive than normal in the last two days.

"I'm doing well, Annie. How are you? And why are you calling me on my office phone? I thought my cell was the first number on my resume."

"I hope you don't mind," she says without missing a beat. "I've learned over the years that I have a harder time reaching people on their personal number during regular office hours. I thought I'd take a chance and grab you here so we didn't waste any more time."

"Oh." I'm a little taken aback by her candor, but not in a bad way. I like that she's so direct. "No, it's fine. I just forgot what it sounded like until it rang."

She chuckles on the other end of the line but then gets right back to business. "Listen, I know it's only been a couple of days since we talked but we were really impressed with you."

"You were?" It's ridiculous to be shocked by the fact that I have the skills she needs. I know I can fill the position she has open. I guess I'm not used to getting a lot of praise for doing my job.

"Absolutely. We need someone with your skillset, but who can also jump in and do other things as well if needed. We're sticklers for our employees taking their vacation time and that means helping each other out at times. It's not every day or even every week. But regularly."

The more Annie talks, the better the job sounds. It was practically a fight with Mrs. Welch to be able to take two days off to see my parents a couple of months ago. It had been well over a year since I'd taken any time off before then. Knowing the Slingers doesn't treat people like that makes it look even more enticing. And makes my heart hurt just a little.

"I'm not going to beat around the bush," Annie continues. "I don't need to see any other candidates. I like you. I think you'll fit right in here. And I have every confidence you can do the job well. What would you think about coming to work for us?"

My mouth gapes open in shock. I knew what she was getting at when she started talking up the company again. But it didn't seem real until the offer finally came out of her mouth.

"I… don't know what to say."

"How about you say yes so we can have you here in two weeks?"

I want to say yes. The work environment alone is so much more positive than what I get working here. Add in the salary and benefits and I'd be stupid not to jump at the chance.

I'm just so afraid of getting myself back into the same situation I'm in now—one where I'm judged by who I'm dating, or maybe more importantly, who I'm broken up with, and am the main topic of the rumor mill in the office. Wouldn't it be better to go somewhere that doesn't have any ties to my romantic life? A place where no one cares who I'm sleeping with and my work is judged by how well I do the job and that's it?

But can I still get all that with the Slingers? I'm just not sure.

I clear my throat from the words that seem to be lodged there. "Um… I don't think I can."

"Oh." She sounds surprised. To be honest, I'm kind of surprised myself. "I was under the impression you were looking to get out of a bad working environment."

"I am. That's… that's true." I feel myself biting my lip, wanting to tell her the whole truth but battling my desire to remain completely professional as well.

"You don't have to tell me, obviously," Annie says. I can still hear the confusion in her voice. "But can I ask why?"

I feel like I owe her an explanation considering I wasted her time with our interview. But maybe if I tell her the whole truth, she'll understand more and we can put this all to rest.

"I'm dating Liam Tremblay."

There. I said it. No, I haven't talked to him in a couple of days, but that doesn't mean I won't talk to him again as soon as I get myself under control more.

Relief floods me as I realize I don't want to break up with Liam. I think I love him. I just need to figure out how to tell him and hope that he'll forgive my childish behavior.

"Our forward?"

"Yes."

She pauses briefly, probably processing this information. "And you don't think you can be professional working for the same organization?"

"It's not that. It's…" I sigh, regretting that I opened this door. I hate that I have to tell her the rest of the truth now. "He told me he saw my resume in your stack last week and when you weren't looking, he put mine on top of the pile. It just seems like he gave me a leg up on the competition and I don't think that's fair."

"Hmm."

What does hmmm mean? I hope I didn't just get him into any trouble.

"Normally I might frown on something like that, but in his defense, I was complaining to him that I needed a good candidate quickly," Annie says dismissively. "In this situation, I feel like he did me a favor."

I shift uncomfortably. That's the exact same thing he said. I'm not sure how to feel about that.

"I know and it was a nice thing he did. Sort of. But we also just started dating and I don't want something like a break-up to cause problems in the workplace. I'm already living through that." I mumble that last sentence to myself but I know Annie caught it.

"Ellery, I'd like to meet with you if that's okay."

"But…" I stutter, confused by what she's asking. "For a second interview? I just turned down your offer."

"I know. I don't mean here at the office. I'd like to meet you for dinner."

Now I'm really perplexed. Is this a friendly invitation or a work thing? And why?

"Really?"

"I think this conversation would be better finished in a neutral location without the fear of a co-worker walking in on it, don't you?"

I can't even imagine what else there would be to say, but I do like Annie a lot. Dinner with her in a friendly capacity would be more fun than going home to an empty apartment. And she's right. The last thing I need is someone overhearing this conversation. I can only imagine the fallout if anyone knew I was searching for a new job.

"Can you meet me at Chez Vie at seven?"

I mentally calculate how far away the newest casual restaurant in French food is. Shouldn't take me too long to get there from here. "Sure. I guess."

"Great," Annie says sounding really pleased. "And Ellery? Don't be late."

TWENTY-SIX
Liam

Sweat is dripping down my back. My breathing is heavy. My legs ache from exertion. My body feels amazing.

My shoulder? Not so much.

"How's it feeling?" Tucker claps me on the back as we waddle on our skates to the locker room.

It was my first day back at full power and I'm discouraged, to say the least. The scrimmage itself was about what I expected. Lots of speed, lots of playful trash talk, lots of skill-building, and lots of body-checks. Admittedly my teammates held back a bit when shoving me into walls in spite of me giving back my no-contact jersey. It pissed me off at first. Now I appreciate it.

I'm not back to normal. Not even close. Very quickly, my new reality is starting to catch up with me and I know deep in my gut no matter how much I try to push it off, my first line days are over.

"It hurts," I admit to Tucker.

The look on his face confirms what I'm feeling. He

knows if I'm going to get back to regular play, I shouldn't have this kind of pain anymore. It's painfully obvious that my playing days are quickly coming to a close. It's only a matter of time and how much torture I'm willing to put myself through.

It doesn't help that Ellery is still ghosting me. She's much more of a logical party in this kind of situation and could help me think it through. But I can't count on her to be a sounding board right now. I'm giving her the space she needs to process my royal fuck up.

Ain't life grand, right now?

"I'm sorry, man. What are you going to do?"

It's the question I have no answer for right now.

Dropping onto the bench, I blow out a breath and begin the tedious process of stripping out of all my gear.

"I don't know. I knew surgery was going to be a long shot. I guess I just didn't expect it to still be causing me this many problems."

He sighs and sits down next to me. I'm suddenly regretting sharing my thoughts. I never know what Tucker's response will be.

"You thinking retirement?"

Okay, maybe I did know what his response would be. But it doesn't make it any less painful to hear.

"I'm not sure I have much of a choice at this point. I can't even get fucking body-checked." The words come out harsher than I intend as I chuck my sweaty jersey into the laundry bin. But I'm so damn frustrated.

Tucker slides on his blade covers and hands me mine to do the same. Probably better if I don't have a weapon attached to my feet while I'm in this kind of mood.

"Wanna know what I think?"

"Not really," I snap. "But I bet you're going to tell me

anyway."

"Testy, testy."

I glare at him, not in the mood for his humor.

"Alright, I get it. My charming wit isn't doing it for you today." He sighs deeply and rests his elbows on his knees. "Listen, I get it. Things aren't going the way you want and you're frustrated."

"That's a serious downplay of the situation."

"Maybe. But did you honestly think you were immune to aging out of the game?"

"Of course not."

"Then what's the deal? Why are you acting like this is such a shock?"

That's the thing he doesn't seem to understand. It's not shock. It's grief.

Holy shit. That's the first time I realized what I'm actually feeling. All this anger and frustration is actually a front for how sad I feel at the loss of this huge part of my life. The part that has defined me for as long as I can remember.

I feel like my body deflates now that I finally put that together.

"I guess I just always assumed I'd be the exception to the rule," I say a little less forcefully now that I can put a name to my emotions.

"Dude. How many times have we had to sit through training sessions where they grill us on the age of retirement and how we need to get all our finances sorted out now? You really thought you were special?"

"How long do you think you have left, man?"

He perks up. "Well obviously, I'm sticking around for at least another decade. But I can skate circles around all you fuckers."

I snort a laugh while he brings it down a notch.

"I hear ya. And I'm sure I'll be as irritable as you when it's my turn," he admits. "Do you know what you need?"

I roll my eyes and get back to stripping off all my gear. "Oh lord. Here we go."

"Don't get all pissy. I have fantastic ideas," he says as I try to walk away. He just follows, even as I strip down and head toward the showers. "You need to call Ellery, have her ditch work, and meet you at home so she can give you a solid rub down, if you know what I mean."

If my shoulder wasn't hurting so badly, I'd run my fist through his face, just to stop that eye waggle if nothing else. Also, because he once again touched on another point of contention in my life.

Pulling on the nozzle, I climb under the cold spray, happy to have the frigid water beating on my back and distracting me from my emotions.

"Can't," I yell through the spray. "She's still not speaking to me."

"Still? Haven't you groveled yet?"

"No. And I'm not going to. She needs space so I'm giving it to her."

He shakes his head in disgust. "Women are so fucking difficult sometimes. This is why I'm single."

"Is it that or because you're standing here watching me shower like a fucking perv?"

Tucker's eyes roll like I'm the one being ridiculous. "Fine. I'll let you get back to your little rinse off, ya prude. But let's go for drinks later. I hear we've got a new recruit coming and I want to see if Dwayne wants some side action on this."

As much as Tucker annoys me sometimes, even I have to admit he's entertaining. Unfortunately, he's also right.

I was so sure I would be the guy who outlived everyone in professional hockey. The one who played well past retirement age and could still demand top dollar for my skills. But those were the starry-eyed dreams of an arrogant kid who had never felt the disappointment of life. And now it's here. The reality of getting older. The midlife crisis when I'm nowhere near middle age.

This is way worse than I expected it to be.

I won't go down in a blaze of glory with a send-off fit for a king and clips of my best moments played on repeat by SportsCenter as they lament my end to the game. No, I will just quietly be moved down the roster until people say things like, "Liam Tremblay? I remember that name. Didn't he play hockey once?"

It's a blow to my ego, but it's also a hard truth I have to face. I may be special to my family, my friends, my fans. But nothing special past that. None of us are. The sooner I can get my brain around that fact, the sooner I can move on with my life and maybe find happiness somewhere else.

That "somewhere" is hopefully in the arms of one Ellery McIlroy, the woman I wasn't expecting but is beyond my wildest dreams.

Turning off the spray, I push thoughts of Ellery out of my mind. Thinking about her makes my chest hurt and I can only handle one pain at a time.

I wrap a towel around my waist and think about what needs to be done. First things first, hit the trainers for a little cupping therapy and maybe a good shoulder rub to get rid of some of the tenderness from overcompensation. Then Coach's office.

I can either do this the easy way or the hard way. But if my shelf life is coming to an end, I should at least know what my options are.

Last, I need to find a way to fix this with Ellery. Because nothing about the word "retirement" sounds good if I don't have her by my side.

TWENTY-SEVEN
Ellery

I've never been to Chez Vie, but now that I'm here, I can see what all the fuss is about. It's not a five-star, sit down for four hours, fancy French restaurant. It's more like a family-friendly place with a mixture of tables and booths, that also happens to serve French food.

I like it. It doesn't feel stuffy or uptight to me. Just an interesting variety on my next meal. It helps that Annie is really relaxing to be with. Not that we've done much talking. We were seated almost immediately and it's been chit-chat about the menu ever since.

"I'm excited to try the Coq Au Vin," she says as she hands her menu to our server who has taken our orders.

"It sounds delicious."

"I promise you won't be disappointed," our server re-assures. "I'll go put the order in now. Let me know if you need anything."

We thank him and he walks away leaving us to what I'm hoping will be a casual conversation.

Annie rests her elbows on the table and leans in. "Let's

talk more about this job."

I figured Annie would eventually get down to business but part of me was hoping she would forget. No such luck.

"We can but I don't really think you'll change my mind."

Clasping her hands together, she leans in closer. "Humor me and let me try."

I smile. Even though this isn't working out, it's still nice to be wooed.

"I just want to know what all the hesitation is about. That's what I can't figure out. From everything you've said, it sounds like you're excited to have a new opportunity. What's really holding you back?"

My smile falls. "I'm trying to leave a company owned by my last boyfriends' mom."

"Ah." She picks up her goblet of water. "And with you dating Liam, you don't want to go to another company where your boyfriend works. This makes more sense now."

Relief floods through me along with a sense of sadness. I'm glad I don't have to spell things out to her. The idea of trying to explain the emotional difficulty of this kind of situation isn't appealing. But that also means she knows there's no sense in trying to convince me to take the job. These kinds of situations almost never end well. As the head of human resources, I'm sure she tries to avoid drama at all costs.

"Tell me about this firm you work for." Annie picks up her napkin and snaps it out before placing it on her lap. "How big is it? How many people work there?"

"At last count, I believe there were twenty-seven full-time employees. Um, I think we have a couple of part-time people as well."

"That's what I thought," she says matter-of-factly. "Do

you know how many employees the San Antonio Slingers have?"

Startled by the question, I quickly tell her the truth. "I wouldn't have any idea."

"When you add in food service, janitorial staff, part-time employees, we're talking thousands."

"Wow. That's large." And my awe in how capable she is in doing such a huge job increases quickly.

"Listen, Ellery, I understand your fear and I'm not try-ing to sway you. Well, maybe a little bit," she admits. "I'm not here as the HR manager. I'm here as a professional woman who sees potential in another professional woman. I want you to have all the information before you pass on what could be a great opportunity for you and your career."

I appreciate her seeing something in me she likes, but I'm still not sure what we're doing here. Still, I owe it to her to listen to what she has to say. I'm getting a French dinner out of it so I might as well. "What information?"

"That you will never, ever see Liam Tremblay at work unless you go looking for him. Or he comes looking for you. But in the halls? I am ninety-nine percent sure it'll never happen because it's never happened to me. Do you know how I got started with the Slingers?"

I shake my head wishing I had done more research on her before my interview.

"Of course, you don't," she says with a wave of her hand. "Because everything was kept on a professional lev-el." Annie shifts in her seat and leans a bit closer like she has a story to tell. "I was dating Ethan Durress. I'm assum-ing you don't know who that is."

"Should I?"

"If you follow hockey you'd know he was our goalie. He dropped my name to the then HR director who liked my resume and hired me. And then Ethan and I broke up."

"Oh no."

She shrugs like the whole situation was just an inconvenience and not what would have been severe heartbreak for someone like me. "That's all water under the bridge now. But it wasn't at first and I suspect back then I thought the same thing as you."

"What's that?" I ask quietly, my heart pounding just knowing she understands my fears as much, or more than I do.

"That we broke up so surely the organization would have to choose between him or me and I was going to be the loser, right?" I say nothing, wanting to hear the rest of her story. "I was wrong. My boss called me into the office, forbid me from pulling Ethan's files under any circumstances, and sent me back to work. A year later, Ethan was traded to Vancouver where he retired."

"Wait…" I'm flabbergasted that she makes it sound so… easy. "That was it? No reprimand or discussion about why inner-office dating is a bad idea?"

"Please. More than a third of people report dating a co-worker at some point. It's not unusual. Now, don't get me wrong, there was more to it on the personal side of course. I was still nursing a wound. But on the professional side? It wasn't that big of a deal. It was just like going to any other job while you're heartbroken. My boss just happened to be signing Ethan's paycheck too."

I think about what all this means. About how Liam and I could work for the same organization but never see each other in the office. About how if we broke up, his payroll could be processed by someone else and I'd never have to pull his files. About how I could work in a job that's supportive and happy to help me through a broken heart versus where I'm at now, where my boss seems determined to keep me unhappy for some reason. Still, I have another question for Annie.

"Why are you telling me all this?"

She thinks for a second before answering me. "I don't want you to miss an opportunity like this one because you think Liam got you the job. Or that Liam will eventually get you fired. Neither is true. The Slingers is a great organization to work for. The salary is amazing, the work environment is relatively drama-free, and you can't beat the medical insurance. And don't get me started on the perks if you're a hockey fan."

"You think I should go for it."

"I think you need to strongly consider how long you want to stay working for your ex-boyfriend's mother and when, or if, you'll ever have a job offer like this again. And I also want you to know, I'm not worried about Liam slipping your resume in. I'm glad he did. I think you're the person we're looking for. You fit every box I want checked for our newest employee, plus some. Your skillset, your personality, even your concern about potentially creating future drama and how it could possibly hurt the work environment."

"When you say it that way, I sound a little ridiculous to have reservations," I say with an embarrassed laugh.

"Not ridiculous. Concerned for your fellow co-workers and their well-being too, which is admirable. All these things show you're exactly right for this job. And I may not have ever found you it if it weren't for Liam."

Biting my lip, I glance down at the table. For all the confidence I've gained over the past few months, I still have a long way to go. But how will I ever gain more, how can I ever really discover who I am if I don't take chances

228

on things I really want? And the truth is, whether Liam was working for the Slingers or not, I really want this job. I want the opportunity to learn from someone like Annie in a place that has coworkers like Jared. I want to try something new and dammit, I want to stop making decisions out of fear.

"Annie, I'd like to change topics please."

Her shoulders slump and her effervescent look deflates just a bit.

"Can we please turn this lovely evening get together into a business meeting?"

She quickly perks up, shoulders straightening as she goes right into boss mode. "Really. What do you have in mind?"

"Let's talk vacation time."

TWENTY-EIGHT
Liam

Sipping on my whiskey, I ignore the sounds of the bar all around me. There's too much on my mind to care about who Dwayne is hustling tonight or which teams are meeting up and blowing off steam together. I have life-altering things happening. Thankfully everyone here seems to be able to read my mood and is giving me a wide berth.

My meeting with my coach went as well as could be expected for someone facing retirement. Not him. Me. It sucks but I appreciate that he's had similar conversations before so he knows how to handle us with kid gloves and give us some dignity at the same time.

Fuck, it sounds like I'm planning end-of-life shit. In a way, it feels like it, too. The only life I've known for the past thirty-one years is almost over. And isn't that just a kick in the gut?

I'm still not sure what my next steps are going to be. There's a lot to work out. I still have a year on my contract so I have some time. Technically I'll still be on the roster and will be required to report to practice, even if all I ever see of game time again is sitting on the bench. That might be the worst part. I won't just be cut and that's the end of it. No ripping off the band-aid for me. I'll have to be there every day watching the younger, faster, healthier guys pass up this old man and take my place.

This is worse than being traded. There are so many decisions to make and so many harsh emotions I'm going to feel, and I don't want to do them alone. Sure, Tucker will support me through it. And coach mentioned a guy who can help make my transition easier by making sure all my financial ducks are in a row. But that's less important to me than having the support of a certain purple-haired pixie.

I could call her, but I promised to give her space and I plan to honor that. Too many people in her life have pressured her into making decisions before she knew what she wanted, and I won't be that person.

Sighing deeply, I bring the tumbler to my lips again, relishing the burn in my gut as I take the final swig of this Johnny Walker Black.

"Need another?"

Paul doesn't wait for my answer, just grabs a fresh glass and pours me three fingers.

"No wonder you own this place," I say keeping my eyes downcast. "I didn't even have to say the word and you've already got me pegged."

He chuckles under his breath and pushes the glass toward me. "That has nothing to do with my bartending skills."

"Then what is it?" I ask and take another satisfying sip.

"You're not the first athlete who sat at my bar looking dejected while his teammates are enjoying themselves." He rests his hands on the bar giving me the impression he's not going anywhere. "Is it your woman or your job that has you giving off a don't fuck with me vibe?"

I huff a humorless laugh. "Both."

"Ouch. Double whammy."

"Yup."

"Or maybe not."

I look up at him, brows furrowed.

He gestures to the front door. "Someone just showed up."

Ellery.

I blink twice to make sure I'm not seeing things but no. She's here. Her lavender hair stylishly spiked, her lips my favorite shade of red. Her black skirt clinging to her body just enough that I can see her shape, but doesn't distract from the killer leopard print heels she's wearing.

Ellery looks around the room before finally catching my eye, a soft smile gracing her lips. Without dropping my gaze, she walks toward me like a woman on a mission. Oh, how I hope that mission is reconciliation.

Finally approaching, she stops just feet from me. "Is this seat taken?"

"I was saving it for you."

With a playful wink at me, she slides onto the stool.

"Nice to see you, Ellery." Paul tosses a napkin on the counter in front of her. "Can I get you something to drink?"

"I think I'm going to stick with water tonight."

He nods and quickly fills a glass. "I'll leave you guys alone. If you need anything, just holler."

"Thanks, Paul."

Turning to face me, she scoots in close and leans on the bar. Taking her cue, I reach up and brush a short lock of hair off her forehead.

"I missed you."

"I missed you, too. And I'm sorry it took me so long to get my thoughts in order. That was... immature of me."

"It's okay. It was stressful, wondering if you'd ever come back to me. But I wanted to make sure it's what you wanted. I never want to push you."

She grabs my hand and slides her fingers in between mine. The warmth of her touch is exactly what I need and I feel a sense of calm come over me. I'm still stressed and sad in some ways, but this makes me feel more centered.

"I love that about you—that you want me to have my own opinions and know what they are. But I still shouldn't have left you like that and not contacted you. It was rude and unnecessary and I'm going to try to do better." She licks her bottom lip before speaking again. "I don't want to have a relationship like that. I want to be an adult. A real adult and be able to talk through problems, even when I'm scared. And I'm going to do my best to trust that you aren't going to push me, and I hope you can trust that I won't ghost you again."

I reach up and pinch her chin between my thumb and forefinger, pulling her toward me. "I do trust you." And then I kiss her. It's the first time since before our fight and it's quick, but it is exactly what I've needed. "And I'm sorry I overstepped with your resume. I didn't even think about what that would feel like to you."

Settling into her seat she takes a sip of her water. "You didn't. You did the same thing any loving boyfriend would do. If it was you, I would have done the same thing. It just spooked me. But when I stopped panicking and got more information about the setup of the office, I realized how it's different working in an organization like the Slingers. It's not at all like working at a firm. And I'm so sorry I accused you of trying to get me in the door. I know that wasn't your intention and I feel so bad to have transferred all my fears onto you."

"Ellery, I need to make something clear. I love you." Her eyes widen. "Yeah, I said it. I *love* you. *You.* I never want to change who you are. I want you to have your own opinions and ideas. You're kind of a free spirit when you want to be and I love watching that part of you."

She shakes her head. "I'm still relatively reserved."

I lean in with a smirk and whisper in her ear. "Unless I'm sucking on that spot on your neck."

A small giggle erupts from her lips. "Yes, until then."

"If you don't want the job, Ellery, don't take it. You're the only one who knows if it'll be a good fit. I personally think it will be, but ultimately it's up to you and I'll support whatever you choose."

"I'm glad you said that because I'm going to need all the support I can get."

Her matter-of-fact tone has me curious about what she's alluding to.

"Why? Did you get another offer?"

"I did. It came with more money and more vacation time."

My eyes widen in surprise. "Really? That's great? Did you take it?"

Ellery straightens, a look of pride written all over her face. "You sir, are looking at the newest payroll manager for the San Antonio Slingers."

"You took the job."

She shakes her head. "I negotiated a better job, as a matter of fact. Because I am worth it."

"Damn right you are." I pull her closer so I can feel her next to me. "I'm proud of you, sweets."

"I'm proud of me, too." She leans in, our lips just a

breath away, and whispers, "Now why don't you finish that drink so we can blow this joint and go celebrate."

I smile and kiss her. It's not hurried. There's no rush to get to the nearest bed so we can maul each other. It's just love. Pure, unadulterated affection for each other and an understanding that even a disagreement won't change our feelings.

Pulling back, Ellery uses her thumb to wipe lipstick residue off my lips. "So, it looks like we're going to be working in the same building, huh? Any chance you'll take me out to lunch?"

The smile on her face has me pushing down the sadness I've been feeling. "I will always take you out to lunch. But only if you want me to. I wouldn't want your boyfriend to accidentally influence your work ethic."

"Smartypants." She nudges my shoulder playfully. "How was practice anyway? Today was your first day of full-contact, right? Did it go well?"

I sigh, my mood plummeting again. Not as low as it was, but it's still hard. Ellery picks up on it immediately.

"Oh no. Was it bad?"

I try to smile. Try to play it off like it's no big deal. But I can tell the forced tip-up of my lips isn't fooling anyone.

"No. It didn't go well."

Ellery's shoulders slump and I know she feels this almost as deeply as I do. "What happened?"

"It just... hurts. The ache in my shoulder is always there and they were careful with me, didn't go all out with body-checks. But one hit and I couldn't move the puck anymore. It's like my shoulder just gave out."

"Oh, Liam." She places her hand on my arm and leans her head on my shoulder. "What happens now? More PT? Or do they just give you more time?"

"Retirement."

She sucks in a breath, eyes wide in shock. "Retire... that's just it? It's over like that?"

"That might be the worst part. I'm medically cleared to play, no restrictions, but we all know I'll never be at one hundred percent again. I can't keep up with my teammates. Hell, I can't even keep up with some of the taxi squad."

"I don't know what that is."

"It's the people I should skate circles around. But I'm not. So, for the next year, I get to report to work every day, knowing I've likely played my last professional game and didn't even know it at the time."

"Oh, Liam." If anyone else said my name in that breathy tone, I'd be convinced they were pitying me. But with her it's different. I know it's a deep sadness for what is slowly being taken from me and the fact that I won't have closure on it for a long time. "What can I do for you? How can I help?"

"Honestly, just you being here is enough."

"I'm sorry I wasn't here earlier so you didn't have to sort through all this alone."

"You're here now. And trust me, we've got plenty of time for you to support me through this transition. Lots and lots of time." I drain the rest of my glass and drop it back down on the bar.

"Wanna take me home so I can help you take your mind off it? There are a lot of things I can do that won't hurt your shoulder."

My eyebrows shoot up at her obvious flirtation. This woman never fails to surprise me. "Yeah? What do you have in mind?"

"I was thinking I could try that thing you liked with my tongue again."

I about swallow mine just thinking about it. "That's uh…" I clear my throat which has suddenly gone dry. "That's quite an offer."

"It's not an offer. It's a promise."

"Bartender!" I yell across the bar. "I need to close my tab!"

Paul shakes his head with a knowing smile but quickly does as I ask. In mere moments, Ellery and I are out the door, headed through the parking lot to my truck.

"I guess we'll pick up my car in the morning again."

"We really need to start planning better."

Ellery giggles and I put my arm over her shoulder, pulling her to me so I can kiss her on the top of the head.

As sad as I am to be retiring, I know deep down it's the right time. When the body calls it quits, there's not much you can do about it except enjoy your final ride. And that's what I intend to do.

Besides, it's not all bad. I've got the woman of my dreams climbing into my truck ready to continue on this journey with me, no matter what job I'm in. And really, there's not much more that I can ask for.

Except maybe a ring. But that'll come. I have no doubt.

TWENTY-NINE
Ellery

Deep breathes, Ellery. You can do this.

Talking to myself isn't working. My stomach is still tied up in knots. Why is this so hard? It's everything I want. I just have to get the strength to do it.

My phone pings with a message, providing a welcome distraction. Even more so when I see it's from my hot boyfriend. The boyfriend who tried really hard to relax me with his tongue this morning. It worked. Temporarily anyway.

> Liam: You can do this. You are strong and deserve to be happy. Go kick some ass.

How in the world he knew exactly what I needed to hear and exactly when is a question I may never know the answer to, but he always does. And while I'm trying really hard not to need him to feel strong, I need him to feel whole.

I guess I just answered my own question as to how he

can read my mind sometimes.

I don't respond, unwilling to waste another few seconds of my life feeling anxious. Instead, I put my phone in the pocket of my dark pink poofy skirt and knock on the door.

"Come in." Her tone is clipped as usual and I stand up straighter, steeling myself for the inevitable verbal smackdown.

Pushing the door open, I step through.

"Good morning, Mrs. Welch. Do you have a minute?" I force a smile on my face, attempting to set the tone for this conversation. By the way her eyes narrow, it doesn't work.

"What do you need Ellery? Is the Knox account giving you trouble? It can be confusing if you aren't used to the various entities they cover."

Their account actually isn't difficult at all. It's one of the easier ones I work with. Not that Mrs. Welch cares. I've realized she regularly greets people with an insult, thinly veiled as a "work issue". Just one of the many things I've discovered about her since I took off my Welch-colored glasses.

Shrugging off her snark, I approach her desk.

"No, that's all caught up." Handing her a single sheet of paper, I continue. "I'm actually here to put in my two-weeks' notice."

Her gaze flips up to mine and I ignore her look of surprise.

"I've accepted a position as the payroll manager for the San Antonio Slingers."

"You're leaving."

The disbelief in her voice should be insulting, but I've also come to realize how self-absorbed she is. Obnoxiously so. That doesn't have anything to do with me, though. It's her own character flaw and nothing I do, good or bad, will change it.

"I am. However, I know there is a process to transfer all my files over to my replacement, so I've negotiated a start date three weeks out instead of the standard two. This will give me a little extra time to make sure whoever takes over my clients is fully trained and there won't be any interruption to their accounts that you'll have to deal with later."

Mrs. Welch drops the paper on her desk and leans forward. "After everything I've done—giving you a job you were barely qualified for, inviting you into my home, allowing you to date my son, you're giving me a standard letter of resignation?"

I startle at her aggressive words. *Barely qualified? Allowed* to date her son? I guess being self-absorbed is a downplay of some serious narcissism.

"I graduated at the top of my class with my degree so I'd hardly say I was *barely qualified* as a junior accountant. And as much as I appreciate you treating me like family…" We both know I'm lying, but it seems like the right way to phrase it in this moment. "… this is an opportunity I can't pass up. Professionally speaking of course."

Mrs. Welch's nostrils flare and I brace myself for whatever she has to say.

"That's fine Ellery. You do what you have to do for *you*. Don't worry about the rest of us. In fact," she places her hands on her desk and pushes to standing. "Let's not worry about training the new person. Consider today your last day. I'll honor your request with paid leave for the next two weeks, but you can go ahead and clean out your desk today."

A year ago, those venomous words would hit their target. I would have been shaken up trying to figure out how to fix this situation. But a lot has happened in the last few months. I've grown up. I'm less worried about what people think of me, especially when the only person they are really concerned with is themselves.

With those thoughts in the back of my mind, I smile back at a scowling Mrs. Welch.

"It seems like this worked out for both of us, then. Thank you for the opportunity to learn more about the industry and myself during my time here."

I turn on my heel and leave her office, head held high, no anxious feelings at all.

Rounding the corner, I prepare to stop at the reception desk. Unfortunately, the last person I want to see is standing right there, chatting her up.

"Ellery," Kevin greets. "How are you?"

I'm confused why he's here. Again. He never stopped in very often when we were together, even when I would beg him to go to lunch, so it's been strange that he seems to pop in all the time now.

"I'm great, thanks. What are you doing here?"

"Oh. Um." he clears his throat. "My mom has some wedding stuff she wants to go over with me."

"Uhhh… shouldn't the bride be here, too?"

"Mom wanted to talk to me about it first."

"Ah." Somehow, I'm not surprised that Mrs. Welch is taking over the nuptials. Looks like I dodged a bigger bullet than I realized. "Well don't let me keep you," I say with obvious indifference. Turning to Brittany I ask, "Do you know where I can get a sturdy cardboard box?"

Her eyes dart back and forth between Kevin and I, like she's waiting for something dramatic to happen. She's going to be sorely disappointed. I'm too interested in getting out of here than to strike up an in-depth conversation with my ex.

"Um… yes. I can go get one for you."

Brittany scurries off leaving me alone with Kevin.

In an attempt to ignore him, I pull out my phone and shoot off a quick text.

Me: Done. And like you predicted, I've been let go with two weeks paid leave. I'm headed home as soon as I pack up.

Liam: You okay with that?

Me: More than okay. Two weeks of vacation before I start my new job just means I can spend a little more time with my new hunky boyfriend.

Liam: Wanna do lunch then? One o'clock? I know this great hockey guy who happens to be a really good cook and finally perfected his zoodles.

Me: Lol. I'll be there.

Clicking my phone off, I put it back in my pocket and look up, almost startled when I see Kevin eyeing me. I'd completely forgotten he was here.

"What's going on, Ellery?" He sounds so concerned.

Like my being happy about making lunch plans is unusual. What is it with this family thinking all my happiness revolves around them?

"What do you mean?"

"Are you cleaning out your desk? Did you get fired?"

I snort a laugh at his ridiculous assumption.

"Of course not. I quit to take a job as the new payroll manager for the San Antonio Slingers."

He blinks rapidly a few times like the idea of another company seeing my value is a shock.

"The hockey team?"

"Yep."

"Are you sure you're ready for that?"

I furrow my brow. "Really, Kevin? No congratulations, just an insult disguised as concern?"

His face begins to redden. "I don't mean it like that. It just sounds like there's a lot at stake if something goes wrong, or whatever."

"It's a good thing I have a fantastic new boss then," I say as Brittany approaches with the box in hand. "She's excited to train me to my full potential. And I'm excited to have mandatory vacation time. Maybe I should go to Maui with Liam. I've always wanted to hike up a volcano."

I need to put that on my bucket list.

Taking the box from Brittany I thank her kindly. Poor girl probably needs a little kindness, considering she's stuck working here for now.

I turn toward my office, looking at my ex one last time, really taking him in. What did I ever see in him? I shake my head once, ridding myself of my own self-doubt.

"Anyway, good luck with your marriage Kevin. Hope it's everything you both dream it to be."

With that, I walk back to my office, a smile on my lips.

I have zero feelings toward this family at all. Not good. Not bad. Complete indifference.

I'm free.

THIRTY
Ellery

3 MONTHS LATER

I practically sprint into the kitchen, putting my hoop earrings on as I go. Well, sprint might be an exaggeration. In my new Louboutin's courtesy of my fabulous new salary, it's more of a quick walk. Regardless, I get there as quickly as I can.

"What are you doing, Liam? We need to leave in a few minutes."

He doesn't look up from his computer, too intent on what he's focusing on. "I'm ready. I'm just trying to fix this edit while I wait for you. Why do I look so shitty on camera? Do I look this bad on television in a jersey, too? Don't answer that. The helmet hides most of my face," he grumbles.

I laugh and kiss him quickly, careful not to leave any lipstick behind. Coral, the tabby kitten Liam got me for Christmas runs over for a quick nuzzle so I pick her up and scratch her behind her ears. I love having my own pet, even if she lives here. But it's better for her to have a friend, and lately I've caught her and Patches napping together. It took a couple of weeks of Patches giving us all the evil eye, but he's finally accepted her as part of the family.

"You look fine. Handsome and sexy as always. You're just not used to seeing yourself on a monitor."

"So, this is what I look like in real life?" The expression on his face is priceless. "That's even worse."

"You look amazing. People are going to love you just like I do. I promise."

"You give me way more credit than you should," he argues with a shake of his head.

Knowing retirement is quickly approaching, Liam decided to start working on the idea of a YouTube channel where he teaches athletes how to make healthy food in the portion sizes they need. Including all the measurements like calories and fat content so viewers can pick and choose based on what part of the season they're in. So far, he's shot three videos so he has content ready to go when he launches the new channel. I think they've turned out fantastic, especially since he's learned how to add words on the screen so people can write down the instructions as he goes. It's really professional and easy to follow. I'm impressed with how much he's learned in a short amount of time. Liam, on the other hand, isn't convinced yet.

Slamming the laptop shut, he huffs and then finds himself distracted. With a raise of his eyebrows, he looks me up and down.

"You look like sex on heels."

I laugh because he always says the sweetest things to me. "I look like I'm going to a baby shower at a bar with all our friends."

He shakes his head slowly. "Not hardly. Those thigh-high boots alone are making me hard. Add those tiny little shorts and I'm ready to ditch the party so I can stay here and bend you over this table."

"First, I'm not wearing shorts. I'm wearing a jump-suit."

"Don't care. I'll be stripping you out of it as soon as possible."

I drop Coral on the floor and she bounds away, probably to pounce on Patches, and put my hands on my hips. "If it helps, it might look sexy now. But just remember, whenever I have to pee, I have to take the whole thing off to sit which looks way less sexy."

"You're trying to make me less horny by reminding me you have to take off all your clothes in public? Bad plan, Ellery."

"Okay, okay. How about this." I turn and pick up a platter off the counter. "You promised to provide the brisket and there is four huge trays Lauren is expecting to be delivered in the next thirty minutes. You really want to piss off Lauren for a little nooky?"

"Yes. Yes, I do." He shoves his keys in his pocket and grabs the largest of the platters so we can load up the car. "But because I'm a man of my word, I'll wait until later."

"Thank you."

"No, thank you. I have all kinds of ideas for later with you looking like that. Please tell me you're wearing a g-string under there."

I stop in my tracks to look over my shoulder, peeking through my lashes. "Who says I'm wearing anything at all?"

Liam throws his head back and groans. "That was so mean, woman. Why doesn't Paul have that kitchen done yet? No one even cares if we're late. They just want the food. I could be getting my rocks off if I'd cooked it there in advance."

"Relax my horny lover. The remodel will be done soon so next time you can ravage me all you want and still honor your commitments."

"Fucking integrity," he grumbles as we load everything into the back of the extended cab and head toward the bar.

Just as I suspect, Liam can't keep his hands off me as we drive. His giant palm keeps finding my thigh and slowly sliding up my shorts as high as he can get until I bat his hand away. He thinks it's funny. Honestly, I do too. I love that he's still so flirty with me and I can turn him on just by wearing what I like. Turns out, my newfound love of fashion has more benefits than just making me feel pretty. I get a lot of exercise in the bedroom, too.

Liam and I aren't officially living together, but we spend more and more time at his house. Yet another reason my first pet lives here. It's not that I don't like my apartment. I do. It just feels different now. I didn't pick it out so I feel like I'm riding out the lease until I can move on and into something I truly want. Something that fits my style. Does that mean Liam's house? I don't know yet. Time will tell if we decide to stay there or if we decide to go house hunting for something we both want. The only thing I know for sure is he's not going anywhere anytime soon. He makes it clear to me every single day that as long as I'm here, so is he. Retired or not.

Turning into the parking lot I know so well now, Liam drives right up to the door and puts his hazard lights on. Carefully, so I can balance on the gravel in heels, I climb out and make my way to the back so I can help carry food inside.

As soon as the front door opens and I get out of the

chilly temps, I hear Lauren squeal.

"Ohmygod Ellery are those red soles on the bottom of those fabulous boots?" She runs over and gasps as she takes in my footwear. Nevermind the fact that I'm holding a giant platter of brisket I need to put down. Nope. Shoes are more important. "Holy shit, you did not spring for thigh-high Louboutin's. How the hell much do they pay you at this job? Do they need an office manager?"

I carefully brush past her before my arms break off from the weight of the platter. "Before you get too excited, I got them second-hand so I didn't even come close to paying full price."

"I don't care." As soon as the food is on the counter and safely out of my arms, she grabs me and spins me around. "And with that jumpsuit, too? Holy shit you look amazing." Lauren pulls me in for a random hug and I hear sniffles next to my ear. "And the student becomes the teacher."

I giggle and pull away from her, needing to continue helping with the unload but as I glance in that direction, it appears the guys have it done already. "You're ridiculous my fashion-loving friend, you know that?"

"I've been called worse," she says with a wave of her hand. "But seriously. You look amazing. And it's not just your outfit. You just sort of glow these days."

I pretend to fluff my super short hair. "Maybe it's because of the new color. You like it tinted a little more pink?"

"I do," she says with a nod. "But that's not why you're glowing. It's because you're in looooooove," she sing-songs.

I shrug playfully but don't deny it. She's probably right. Liam has been so good for me. He makes me feel confident and sexy. But more important, he makes me feel valued. And that's the best feeling of all.

People continue to trickle in as Lauren, Kiersten and I decorate and set up for the shower. Our significant others are supposed to be helping but are they? No. They're too busy checking out the kitchen remodel and discussing Liam's new venture. I could be mad that they're being lazy bums but in all honesty, I'm thrilled to have "couple friends".

I've always felt just slightly out of place, like I'm on the periphery of relationships, watching as people have strong bonds with everyone else but me. Now, everything is falling into place. I have a boyfriend I love more than I thought possible, I have solid friends who include me in their plans, I have a job I'm excited to go to every day, and Kevin? Honestly, I have no idea. The minute I quit my old job, I dropped that entire part of my history, not even caring to look back.

He's tried calling me a couple of times but I haven't bothered to answer. Why should I? I have nothing to say to him at all and I finally realized, I don't owe him an uncomfortable conversation that leaves me feeling yucky. I owe it to myself to focus on my new life.

I can honestly say I'm happier than I've ever been. I just had to drop some of my reservations and start the journey to becoming who I'm supposed to be. I'm still not there yet, but I'll get there eventually. It's a journey I hope to continue on for as long as I can.

My friends and I continue making sure everything is in place for the party of the year with minimal prodding towards the men. Well, minimal for me, anyway. Lauren finally threatened to do a striptease and then make Heath sleep on the couch if he doesn't hustle more. Unsurprisingly, it works. Eventually, everything is set up and the door opens, the family of the hour strolling in... all dozen or so of them.

Truly. Both Jaxon and Annika's entire family all try to crowd through the door at the same time.

"Ohmygod you are so cute," Lauren squeals and rushes to a very pregnant Annika, who looks equal parts cute and pissed that she can only waddle across the room.

Jaxon, on the other hand, is clearly delighted at the fact that he's going to be a dad in three months or less. With his arm protectively around his wife, he practically glows more than she does.

But they're not who stops half the room in their tracks. It's Jaxon's dad that has all the men doing a double-take.

In the entranceway stands Jason Hart, retired defensive lineman, and legend in the world of football. Or so I've been told. I knew Jaxon a bit in college but I had no idea his father was some big-time football player until recently when Liam put the family tree together. Ever want to see a grown man be reduced to a puddle of fangirl? Tell him one of the guys he's been hanging out with and getting to know has a Hall of Fame trophy in his father's den somewhere.

Yeah. I had to hear about that for days and fielded lots of questions like, "Why didn't you tell me?" My answer of course was, "I don't follow sports." Eventually, he let it go. Probably until now.

Feeling said boyfriend approach behind me, I turn just in time for him to kiss me on the cheek.

"You ladies did a nice job with this party."

He slides his arms around my waist and I lean into him.

"You did a nice job with the food." Gesturing to the crowd of people in front of us, I ask, "You sure you don't want to go meet Jaxon's dad?"

"There's time for that later. Besides, he's not the guest

of honor. It would be rude to make this party about him."

"You can't figure out what to say without sounding like a super fan, can you?"

"I'm a professional athlete. We don't super fan." Liam pinches my side making me giggle. "Also, yes. I haven't been this nervous since waiting for scouts to show up at a high school game."

I swivel in his arms and reach up to give him a quick peck. Of course, he has to meet me halfway. Even with four-inch heels on I'm still significantly shorter than him. "You're cute when you're trying not to fangirl."

He slaps my rear playfully and as much as I'm enjoying being with him, I have a job to do.

Annika is already seated in the place of honor with a dark-headed kiddo's hands on her protruding stomach when I reach her. I give her a quick side hug so I don't interrupt the moment.

"You look so great. How are you feeling?" I ask as she runs her hands over Carson's dark hair. He doesn't even look up, too intent on trying to feel the baby kick.

"Kind of like a whale, but I guess it's for a good reason so I shouldn't complain." Annika looks me up and down. "Damn girl, you look freaking amazing. Don't stand too close. I look frumpy next to you."

"You look like you're bringing new life into the world," I say through a laugh. "Nothing looks better than that. Did you guys get the job situation worked out?"

That was one of the hardest things for Annika when she found out she was pregnant. How was she supposed to continue her job as a trainer for the San Antonio Steer and be a new mom at the same time? Based on the look in her eye, though, I'm pretty sure she's figured it out.

"I think we did."

Cocking my head, I refuse to let her get away with half the information. "What? Why do you look like the cat that ate the canary?"

She glances around quickly. "I'm almost positive we're stealing Nicole away from here to be our nanny. It's not set in stone yet, but it looks that way."

"Oh, how fun. She's so great."

"And she's Kade's girlfriend so it's basically a family member caring for my child. That just feels better, you know?"

I don't, being that I've never been in the situation, but I can imagine.

"Anyway," Annika continues. "She hasn't told Paul yet so I probably shouldn't have said anything in front of this one." She gestures toward Carson who's still staring at her stomach intently.

"I don't think he's paying attention."

"Yes, I am," Carson blurts out. "But I don't care where any of you work." His eyes suddenly go wide and he gasps quietly. "Was that the baby or did you fart?"

Annika and I burst out laughing as he moves his hands around, trying to feel whatever it was again.

"It was the baby, Carson," she says through another giggle.

"Are you sure? That was a pretty weak kick."

Still laughing, I stand back up to leave them to it. "I'm going to leave you two to sort this out. I think one of the hors d'oeuvres stations needs a refill."

"Okay but I want to hear about your new job later," she calls after me. "I need to know if you have better perks and I should change organizations."

"We'll compare notes later."

I give her another quick hug and go about my way,

making sure food hasn't run out and drinks don't need to be replenished. We may be having the baby shower at Frui Vita, but the bar is closed. No one is working except the hostesses.

Actually, that means me. No one is working except me. I don't mind, though. Replenishing the mimosa pitcher means I get to take a breather and look around at this amazing friend group of mine. Lauren is chatting up Jaxon's mother and Kiersten is trying to explain to Carson that no, Annika didn't fart. Babies just feel weird when they move in utero.

And then my eyes latch onto Liam. His tall, broad frame fits right in next to his football hero that he's finally had enough nerve to go talk to. His oversized smile as they no doubt talk shop could light up this whole room.

And when he glances around the room, doing a double-take as he catches my eye, he winks. And my heart melts. Never did I think a man like Liam could love a woman like me, but he does. Every single day he shows me exactly how much.

It's wild to think, a year ago, I was passively sliding through life, making decisions based on what other people wanted. And today, I have everything I never realized I needed and so much more.

EPILOGUE
Jason

Standing at the high-top table, sipping on my whiskey, I take a moment to take it all in.

My wife, chatting up our daughter-in-law and one of her friends. My daughter ribbing her big brother over God knows what, entertaining several of the guests. And Jaxon... the boy who made me a father, beaming over the future and the birth of his first child.

I still remember that sad little boy who was so excited when I visited his school on his birthday, and the friendship that turned into so much more. I have vivid memories of him in that hospital bed on the verge of death as his mom and I prayed for a miracle. I will never forget when that miracle was born and how one unplanned baby pulled our entire family together and saved his brother's life.

And here I am, all these years later, with a beautiful wife I'm still madly in love with, three healthy children, and my first grandbaby on the way. It's crazy how fast the years pass by and yet, I wouldn't have changed a thing. Not one thing.

A slap on the back pulls me out of my memories.

"Shouldn't you be sitting at the bar?" Deuce asks. "I hear grandpas are prone to broken hips if they fall."

"You make fun of me now, my friend, but I see Trace over there eyeing up one of Jax's med school friends. Your turn is coming."

"Man, he just turned twenty-one. Give him some time."

"Jaxon met Annika when he was twenty-one. Look around you, brother. See where we are now?"

My best friend for the last two decades glances around the room before a menacing stare falls onto me. "Don't be trying to marry my kid off yet."

"I'm not. I'm just telling you it's coming. We are getting old."

"I don't know who you think is getting old but I could still take you," Deuce grumbles into his drink. For whatever reason, he's decided mimosas are his beverage of choice today. I don't get it, but this is Deuce we're talking about. I learned long ago not to question things.

"Please. You couldn't take me when we were their age."

"Those are fighting words, my friend."

"Make sure Vanessa has the essential oils ready for you after I kick your ass, you pussy."

He gapes at me. "Don't bring my Little Mamacita's side biz into this. You haven't lived until you've rolled some lavender oil on your feet before going to bed at night. You'll sleep like a baby is what you'll do."

"I'm good, thanks," I say with a laugh. "I actually don't think I mind getting older."

Deuce furrows his brow and raises his girly champagne glass to his lips again. "I feel like you've been having some deep thoughts over there, grandpa, so hit me. Why don't you mind getting older?"

I shrug. "I just feel like I'm a better person now. Like age and experience has chilled me out."

Deuce snickers. "How so? You still take on too many projects, are a helicopter parent at all Matty's games, and let's not even talk about how your head almost exploded when that boy asked Lucy to be his girlfriend."

"She is in 8th grade. There will be no boys at least until high school. Or ever."

"Oh yeah. You're so much more chill now. Can't wait for you to be a helicopter grandpa," he says sarcastically.

"Nah. I know I'm a shit father."

"Aren't we all at times."

"Ain't that the truth. But for all my failings as a dad, I feel like I'm gonna be a kick-ass Papa. Something about it feels different."

"You mean the part about spoiling your grandbaby rotten and then sending him home for his parents to deal with?"

I tilt my glass toward him. "That would be the part. It's going to be fantastic."

Before he can respond—but really, what else is there to say?—someone begins clinking their glass, signaling it's time for a toast.

As conversations start to wane, I quietly turn to Deuce. "Have you met Heath Germaine yet?"

"The dude clinking the glasses? Yeah. He's a good guy. Fucking phenomenal running back."

"No shit. What I wouldn't have given to play with someone like him back in the day."

"Amen to that."

"I know toasts aren't typical during a baby shower." Heath's opening statement is met with some chuckles from around the room. "But if you had seen how much work some of the lovely women in this room put in to make this event special, you'd know why it had to be done. Lauren, Kiersten, Ellery, can you please wave so everyone knows who you are?"

The three young women, one with pinkish hair who looks very embarrassed to be called out, all wave to the small crowd.

"What about me?" someone yells from across the room.

"You own this place, Paul. Using your key to let us in doesn't count."

Amid more laughter, Heath takes a few steps to the side and suddenly I know we're about to have more of a show than anyone here realizes.

"I also want to give everyone a friendly reminder that this is a social media free party. Meaning until the guests of honor post pictures on their social media about this event, please don't post any pictures on yours."

"Damn," Deuce murmurs. "I'm so glad we didn't have to have disclaimers at our parties when we were playing."

"We did. You just didn't care."

His glass stops halfway to his mouth. "Oh yeah, I guess that's true."

I turn back to Heath with a shake of my head. We may be older, but Deuce's sense of humor never changes.

"I need to quickly apologize for hijacking this party," Heath continues. "But I have gotten permission from the guests of honor. Jaxon, if you wouldn't mind holding my drink."

Jaxon grabs the glass while Annika looks on with a smile.

"Oh shit," Deuce whispers. "Is he about to do what I

think he's about to do?"

"Yup."

Sure enough, Heath drops to one knee in front of Lauren, whose hands immediately cover her mouth while the rest of the guests gasp and squeal.

"Lauren Bagley..."

Another rumble of excitement goes through the crowd.

"Looking back on the last few years," Heath continues. "I don't know how I ever did life without you. I was a blind fool to not see what was right in front of me all those years. But I see you now. I see you and I appreciate you and I love you deeper than I knew was possible."

"More than football?" someone yells making everyone laugh.

Heath drops his chin to his chest briefly before looking back up. "More than football. More than the 2006 AFC championship when the Colts came back from a 21 to 3 deficit and beat the Patriots to get into Peyton's first Super Bowl."

Everyone laughs at Heath's quip, including Lauren who responds with "You're such a romantic, baby." She's being a good sport about the tangent this proposal is taking.

"That's a lot of love," Deuce says to me. "I don't even know if I love my kids that much."

I snicker but keep my eyes on the almost engaged couple.

"Okay, okay." Heath holds his hand up to quiet the crowd. "Now what was I saying?"

"You love me more than football," Lauren blurts out, eyes still wide.

"I knew you'd know, baby. I love that you keep me on my toes and life never gets boring with you. I love that you keep me on track and that you understand the stressors of my job and always roll with the punches that go along with it. I love that you don't take my shit or placate me and are the first one to tell me to get out of your way because you have shit to do."

"Are you still talking about the bathroom paint color?" Lauren interrupts. "It was floor exercise day at the gym. You know how much I love tumbling. I didn't have time to discuss decorating."

"I will never let it go because it's just another example of how you don't take my shit. Baby," Heath reaches his hand out and Jaxon slaps a small black box in his open palm. Heath opens it and presents it to her, eliciting another gasp. "I never, ever want this to end. I know you don't care about marriage but I do. And I want to stand up in front of God and everybody and tell the world we're forever. Will you please do me the honor of marrying me?"

"It would be my pleasure," she says and cups his cheeks, kissing him. But that's not the end of the smoochy time. As soon as he puts the ring on her finger and stands up, she launches herself at him, wrapping her legs around his waist to keep with the tonsil hockey.

The crowd cheers at the public display of affection until someone finally yells, "Get a room!"

Things begin to die down and Deuce slaps me on the back again. "Welp, I see the little missus is getting teary over that impromptu proposal so my duty as husband calls. Are we still on for dinner tonight?"

"Yep. Reservation for twelve at seven."

"Sounds good. I'm already starving. These finger foods aren't cutting it, man."

He wanders away, still grumbling about how empty his stomach is. I, on the other hand, can't keep my eyes in one place. Looking around the room, I marvel at the family-like relationships Jaxon has made over the years and how it's growing. He reminds me so much of me at that age, I know I must have done something right.

As I continue to stand on the periphery just observing, a guy with floppy blond hair walks by with his phone stuck to his ear. "What do you mean I've been traded? To where? Florida? What the fuck is in Florida?"

I shake my head at the poor sucker as he storms out the front door into the parking lot, which is no doubt quieter than in here. I remember the shock from my teammates whenever they got the call that they were being traded to another team and their life had been upended. But they were always fine. And he will be, too.

My chapter may be over, but the story never will be. Life will continue to march on. I just have to always remember to enjoy where I'm at so I don't miss a thing.

Like the look on my beautiful wife's face as she cradles our daughter-in-law's stomach.

Never did I think when I walked into that elementary school that my life would have such a ripple effect and end up affecting so many of the lives in this room, even indirectly. And to think, it all started because one self-absorbed man lowered his pride, got over himself, and had a change of heart.

I'm so glad I did.

THE. END.

BUT WAIT!

You didn't think that was the end of Tucker, did you? That he would get traded and we never know what happens to him? No way, my friend! Check this out.

UNDER FIRE

SNEAK PREVIEW

Florida can suck it.

I've been here two months and I haven't found one good thing about this place yet.

The mosquitos are the size of vultures only they don't wait until you're dead to attack. The same fucking alligator likes to interrupt my afternoon commute every day and no one has figured out how to relocate him. Some dude got naked on the roof of the local Publix and peed all over the parking lot mere minutes before I got there to do my shopping. And it rains ninety-five percent of the time.

Maybe ninety-five percent is a slight exaggeration, but no shit, the humidity here is unreal. I should be used to it. It's not like San Antonio is dry, but something about it raining so much keeps this place damp as hell. Even my hair frizzes and no one has ever mistaken me for having so much as a wave in this mop.

The only thing I have enjoyed is the regular outings my new teammates have set up.

They're a good group of guys. Mostly everyone is single, being that it's a pretty young team, so no one ditches our bonding time to go home to a wife or girlfriend. Unlike that fucker Liam Tremblay at the Slingers who became somewhat of a buzz kill once he got himself a steady girlfriend.

Speaking of, I should probably call him and see if he can try making a smoked turkey on his new YouTube channel. He's got some good recipes on there, but I could use a little help with my new smoker.

Slamming my car door, I make my way to the entrance of the most opulent building I've seen in this part of Tampa so far. Not that I should be surprised. Hiltons aren't known for being shabby.

I'm greeted by a valet who holds the door open for me.

"Honeysuckle Bar and Grill?" I ask as I step inside the air conditioning.

He points across the huge lobby. "All the way past check-in and take a right."

"Thanks so much."

I start to feel a little more in my element the closer I get to my destination. I could use a night out with my new buddies to take the edge off of my game. We're starting to work together well on the ice, but it's taking some time to gel. That's part of why I never say no when someone suggests an outing. The more we know each other off the ice, the better we'll communicate on it.

Also, I just never say no when someone suggests an outing. I'm too much of a social butterfly.

Entering the small venue, I take a quick look around and almost immediately find who I'm looking for. It's not hard to spot the huge guys taking up almost the entire back of the room. The poor business dudes sitting at the bar who came here looking for a hook up appear awfully dejected knowing all the ladies are looking at the wall of men in the back instead.

What can I say—us hockey players are hot.

"Hey! You made it!" my buddy Maksim Ivanov greets, arms wide like he's going to come in for a hug. If a table full of beer and half-eaten appetizers wasn't in his way, he probably would. Maks has lived in the States since he was a little kid, but still claims the parts of Russian culture he thinks make the most impact. Like kissing your teammates in celebration.

Frankly, I think he's just seeing how much shit he can get away with, but I humor him because... well mostly for the same reason he does it. The reaction we get when I don't act like he's weird cracks me up.

"Of course, I made it." I grab his hand, intertwining our thumbs because that's as close as we're going to get to each other with all these people around us. "You think I would miss checking out the place you picked for us to hang tonight? It's nice."

It's no Frui Vita, but it has its charms.

"Of course, it is! Nothing but the best for us!" He turns and gives flirty eyes to some chick that's hanging all over him. "Nothing but the best for all of us."

I can see they're about to maul each other with their tongues so that's my cue to get out of dodge.

"What are you drinking, Ivanov? Looks like you need a refill."

Only the thought of free booze can pull Maks away from the possibility of immediate sex, even if it's just a temporary distraction.

"Vodka. Beluga Gold if they have it."

I shake my head. Of course, he'd choose the most expensive brand when I'm picking up the tab.

I push through the crowd and head toward the bar and

flag down a bartender. She looks up at me, a smile on her face that immediately falls as soon as she sees me.

That was weird.

I glance around, wondering if she was actually looking at someone behind me, but no. It was me that gave her that sour puss reaction.

I settle in and wait for her to take my order.

And wait.

And wait.

And finally, I flag her down again. She huffs, clearly irritated by me but I have no idea what I've done. I just got here.

She finally approaches, her blonde hair pulled back in a sporty ponytail, her black and white uniform crisp and clean. She looks vaguely familiar but I can't figure out why. The look on her face isn't at all the friendly expression I would expect from a place like this.

"What do you want?"

I'm taken aback by her aggressive tone, but I play it off. Maybe she's having a frustrating night or I remind her of someone she hates.

"Um… do you have Beluga Gold?"

One of her eyebrows rise. "Big spender, aren't you?"

"It's for my buddy over there. I just want a beer. Whatever you have on tap."

She rolls her eyes and walks away without any indication she heard me. But I watch as she gets the vodka off the shelf so I assume I'm still going to be served.

Leaning against the bar while I wait, I turn around to see Maks's tongue practically down that same woman's throat. I chuckle to myself. I should have known it wouldn't take him long. If her wandering hands are any indication, I may end up shooting this vodka by myself when they take off and get a room.

I hear the slam of a mug being forcefully placed on the counter behind me. Sure enough, half my beer has spilled over the rim.

As the pissy bartender grabs a shot glass and begins filling it with Maks's liquid gold, I grab my credit card. She doesn't make any eye contact with me, just treats me like a pest. I'm so confused but feel like I need to get to the bottom of this.

"Um… Miss?"

She finally looks up, still annoyed but at least I'm getting a response.

"Have I done something to make you mad?"

Her nostrils flare and her eyes narrow. "Really? You're seriously asking me that?"

The longer this goes on, the more my head spins. "Really." Then it hits me. "Oh boy. You used to work at that sports bar over on West Main, didn't you? Listen, I'm so sorry if I didn't tip you enough. My friend Maks there," I gesture over my shoulder and Don Juan himself, "he drug me out that night before I could add anything to the tip jar. But I'll make it up to you tonight. I promise."

If it's possible, the look of anger on her face gets even more severe. She huffs a humorless laugh before finally looking at me dead in the eye. "Fuck off, Tucker."

I'm not sure which surprises me more — that she knows my name, or that she throws a twenty-dollar shot in my face before storming off.

Under Fire, the first book in the brand-new Florida Glaze series is coming next year!

www.authormecarter.com/under-fire

ABOUT THE AUTHOR

ME Carter didn't set out to write a book. She just had a random story rolling around in her head after working with her local PTA. Then one day, it became all-consuming and had to be written down. This should come as no big surprise since she has always had random stories rolling around in her head.

She lives in Texas with her four children, Mary, Elizabeth, Carter and Bug. Get it? ;)

You can follow her on Facebook at **www.facebook.com/authorMECarter**, on Instagram, or her website **www.authormecarter.com**.

Want to keep up with all things M.E. Carter? Sign up for her newsletter and read Juked for free! (**www.authormecarter.com/newsletter**)

Other books written by M.E. Carter can be found here. (**www.authormecarter.com/reading-order**)

OTHER BOOKS BY M.E. CARTER

Hart Series
Change of Heart
Hart to Heart
Matters of the Hart
Matters to Me
Matters to You
Matter of Time

Texas Mutiny Series
Juked
Groupie
Goalie
Megged
Deflected

#MyNewLife Series
Getting a Grip
Balance Check
Pride & Joie
Amazing Grayson

Charitable Endeavors
(Collaborations with Andrea Johnston)
Switch Stance
Ear Candy
Model Behavior
Better than the Book

Smartypants Romance
Weight Expectations
Cutie and the Beast

Weights of Wrath

Collaborations with Sara Ney
Friend Trip
Kissmas Eve
New Years Steve

CPSIA information can be obtained
at www.ICGtesting.com
Printed in the USA
BVHW041530301121
622873BV00011B/624

9 781948 852340